CAMBRIDGE AT CHRISTMASTIME

Cambridge at Christmastime

Rainy Day Writers
Cambridge, Ohio

Cambridge at Christmastime
ISBN-13: 978-1466368736
ISBN-10: 146636873X

CONTENTS

CAMBRIDGE CITY SCHOOLS
6111 FAIRDALE ROAD
CAMBRIDGE, OHIO 43725
740-555-4321

November 1, 2011

Dear Valued Graduate:

Cambridge City Schools would like to invite you to participate in the Southeastern Ohio Symposium for Global Travel on December 27-28 at the Pritchard Laughlin Civic Center here. Your expertise in travel and work abroad will be invaluable to 125 seniors from six area high schools who have shown an interest in working and traveling outside the United States. These students are the best and brightest in this area.

While this endeavor is scheduled during the Christmas holidays, it is a chance for those of you who have not experienced Cambridge at Christmastime in recent years to renew old friendships and enjoy how the city comes to life during that special time of the year.

For the all-day sessions on December 27, we suggest you present a 25-minute talk on some of your observations. This should include the do's and don'ts of overseas living. We have scheduled the entire day on December 28 for one-on-one question-and-answer sessions and short slide presentations.

Congratulations on your successful career. We hope to receive an RSVP from you soon.

Yours truly,

Dennis Corvette

Dennis Corvette
Superintendent of Cambridge City Schools

The Eye of the Needle

(Matt. 19:16-24)

Jerrod Michaelson pushed his paperwork away. Stretching his fingers, he studied his hands thoughtfully. Soft, well-manicured, pampered, they hadn't seen physical labor since shortly after he graduated from Yale with degrees in engineering and environmental design.

Sunlight streamed through windows surrounding the massive walnut desk, flashing off the large oval-cut ruby on his left hand. Set in heavy 14-carat white gold and flanked by six half-carat diamonds, the heirloom had been given to him by his grandfather on the Wall Street debut of Michaelson & Associates.

A jagged scar cut across two knuckles, a reminder of the night after that final argument with Elise, when he had slammed his hand in the door of his pride and joy, a 1979 red Mercedes Benz 300D. He felt a twinge from the arthritis setting into the bones of his fingers. Absentmindedly, he rubbed the warm ears of the aging Irish setter affectionately nuzzling his leg. Cash was his constant companion.

"Here's this afternoon's mail, Jerrod." Susan, his long-time secretary, pointed to an envelope with a Cambridge, Ohio, return address. "You'll be particularly interested in this one."

"Thanks," he responded. His voice was deep and clear. "It's from Cambridge City Schools. I haven't been home in twenty-five years. Do you suppose they've tracked me down for an overdue library book after all this time?" They both laughed.

"Well, I'd better get back to work," sighed Jerrod. "Would you see that I'm not disturbed for an hour?"

Slipping the letter from the envelope, he murmured, "Hmm, Southeastern Ohio Symposium for Global Travel. Impressive title. Look at that—signed by Dennis Corvette! He taught school back then. A firebrand, but he got things done. I always admired that. Now he's superintendent. I wonder if he still wears that handlebar mustache."

He studied the letter. *Maybe I'll attend—check out the old stomping grounds, see who's still around. Might run into Elise, though she's probably got kids in college now. She always wanted children…that was a dream we didn't share.*

Life had been good to him, no doubt about that. With a flourishing global business; a luxury penthouse in Manhattan; custom-built homes in Newport Beach, Milan, and Martinique; three sailing vessels; his new Mercedes Benz SL-Class SL65AMG roadster; a private jet, and more money than even he knew what to do with, he had all he'd ever dreamed of, except for one thing…how did that old Beatles tune go? The melody spun tauntingly through his head:

Can't buy me love, love; can't buy me love.
I'll give you all I got to give if you say you love me too.
I may not have a lot to give, but what I got I'll give to you.
I don't care too much for money; money can't buy me love.

Wearily, he leaned back. The soft weathered leather of the custom-designed chair creaked companionably. Jerrod's eyes traveled thoughtfully around the massive office, lighting briefly on the trappings of the good life. A handful of his favorite masterpiece paintings, collected over a lifetime of careful and costly acquisition, tastefully adorned the walls. Built-in display cases held valuable collections from exotic locations. The door frame and crown molding, elaborately hand-carved by commissioned artisan, heavily symbolic of Jerrod Michaelson, spoke volumes about the man, his power, influence, and wealth. But today, it all faded from his awareness as he slipped into a reminiscent reverie.

Growing up near Cambridge had been a wonderful time. The eldest of four kids, he helped his parents on the farm from the time he turned six. Chores grew as the boy grew, beginning with easier tasks like fetching cows in for milking and working in the family garden.

Before daylight, he checked and reset the traps he counted on for spending money. Then there were chores with his dad. Milking, feeding animals, mucking out stalls, repairing equipment, putting up hay, mending fences; he grew up lean and strong, tanned and happy. At night he went to bed bone tired, with a sense of accomplishment but yearning for some indefinable more. His family never had much, but their endowment of a strong work ethic had been a good upbringing.

From the time he was nine, Jerrod had driven tractors, trucks, anything that needed driving. Miley Peterson said, “You git up there and drive that truck, boy. You can do it.” He could barely see above the dashboard. The gas pedal was missing; only the lever was left. After quickly wearing a hole through the sole of his boot, he devised a makeshift pedal from an old boot heel. *Guess that’s where my interest in engineering started.*

He remembered fishing, rabbit and coon hunting with his friends; the companionship of his beagle pup, Peppy; he and his dad taking cows to the Barnesville auction house or visiting the feed store in Cambridge to sell corn, oats, or wheat and carefully carrying home cheeping baby chicks. *I almost smell them now.*

The occasional movie at the State Theatre or shopping trip to Robert’s Men’s Shop or Alexander’s Shoes was a good excuse for a trip to town too. Cambridge was small, but it filled the heart and mind of this hard-working, ambitious country boy with visions of the big city and success. He wanted it all.

When Jerrod turned sixteen, Dad gave him the old black four-door Chevy. He and his buddies had good times in that old stallion. His first kiss was from Ginny Abramson as they sat close together in the front seat. He escorted Elise Anderson to the prom in it—the beginning of the love of a lifetime. When he went to college, he drove the old car to Connecticut. It carried him faithfully back and forth for two years. When it had finally cruised its last mile, he regretfully parked it behind the barn and started riding the bus.

Jerrod sat bolt upright. *The bus. The last time I saw her, she was leaving on the bus.* Remembering the tears on her cheeks as she waved goodbye, he suddenly realized where his thoughts had led. Elise still meant more to him than he'd ever thought possible. But too many years had passed. *She's been over me for a long time*, he thought ruefully.

No, life hadn't given him a hard road. *Except for loving Elise*, he sighed. Nothing filled the void that she'd left in him. The one thing he wanted most was the one thing he might never have.

A tear escaped, trickling down the crease of his cheek. Could he change, find her, make amends? He'd procrastinated too long. *Even if Elise is lost to me forever, I need to see her again and know that I tried. I'm the proverbial rich man trying to go through the eye of the needle, but it's the only way this old heart will ever find any peace.* His resolve set, he reached for the phone. He had much to do.

Jerrod jumped off the sleek Greyhound in Cambridge on a bright sunny winter afternoon. It was a bit nippy, but a beautiful day. Four inches of snow blanketed everything in sight; only the roads were clear. The old bus depot was no more, he'd learned, but he'd decided to ride the bus to prove to himself that he had truly changed. Years earlier, Elise had taken that same difficult ride. It seemed a fitting way to begin his own road home. He had other reasons to keep his arrival low-key too.

The driver pointed out the Comfort Inn. After settling in to a room with a view of I-70, he filled Cash's food and water dishes and watched the dog gulp everything down. Then he coaxed, "Come, Cash. Let's walk off that long ride."

Southgate Parkway was nothing like he remembered it—businesses lined the road as far as he could see in either direction. *Funny, it never occurred to me that Cambridge would ever change*, he marveled.

The old setter cavorted like a pup in the fresh snow, rolling and tumbling, full of life. Snugging his jacket collar around his neck, Jerrod got his bearings and trudged north, taking everything in. *I'm bound to find something familiar eventually*, Jerrod thought. *Surely not everything's changed.* On a small bridge, he watched the shallow icy flow ripple beneath his feet.

"Well, Wills Creek is still here," he affirmed to the snowy-coated dog prancing around him. "Right where I left it. Muddy as ever, but still beautiful in its own way." His breath froze in the air as he spoke.

Continuing toward town, a car rental sign caught his eye. He turned in, tromping toward the office, his boots caked with ice. A youngish-looking man, slipping a coat on, stepped out to greet him. "Fine weather we're having, if you're a penguin! Hi! I'm Christian. Don't get many walk-ins here, especially this time of year. Looking for a rental?"

"Hi! Nice to meet you, Christian. I'm Jerrod. Yes, I need something with room for my dog where he can't get into any trouble." Cash seemed to grin mischievously as he vigorously shook snow from his coppery fur. "We'll need it for two weeks."

"I can fix you up. This little Ford pickup should do the job, don't you think? It has a dog safety feature that'll keep him safe and we can slip a cap onto it if you like."

"Sounds good," Jerrod agreed. "Say, you'd surely know. Is Coney Island still in business?

Turning the truck off the icy lot onto Southgate Parkway a half hour later, Jerrod found himself entering familiar territory. The Guernsey County Courthouse loomed ahead, imposing as ever. The Cambridge he remembered was still here after all.

Cruising the downtown area, he motored west on Wheeling Avenue, cutting north to Steubenville Avenue to Clark Street then back on Wheeling to complete the loop. It felt good to be home. *The downtown area has a wonderful Christmas spirit to it*, marveled Jerrod. *And the Dickens tableaus are terrific.*

He parked by Coney Island, now renamed Theo's; put a leash on Cash; and set out on a walking tour of Wheeling Avenue. Robert's and Casey's were both gone. *My goodness, has it really been that long?* Jerrod shook his head. *So much I've missed.* The State Theatre, to his relief, was still there, but was now a Masonic lodge. As he and Cash strolled along, he read placards describing the Dickens characters, listened to Christmas carols piped into the streets, peeked into shops decorated in season finery, and worked up a ravenous appetite.

Tethering Cash safely in the truck, Jerrod pulled the door to Theo's restaurant open and ran head-on into a man with an unmistakable white handlebar mustache.

"Dennis? Dennis Corvette?" Jerrod stuttered, surprised.

"Yes, how do you know…wait, is that you, Jerrod? My gosh, we've gotten old, haven't we?" Dennis chuckled. "Welcome to Cambridge! I was hoping you'd come for the symposium. What have you been up to, old friend?"

"Well, join me and we'll talk while I eat dinner. I'll buy you a beer for old time's sake," Jerrod grinned. "I haven't eaten since breakfast and I could swallow an elephant whole."

"Well, Steve doesn't have elephant on the menu, but everything at Theo's is delicious. I highly recommend the fish and chips."

Shortly, settled at a table near the bar, Dennis studied Jerrod's face while he sipped his beer. "You have that look in your eye, Jerrod," he asserted. "I've seen it before. You're not here just for the symposium, are you? You're up to something. Spill it."

"I never could get anything by you, Dennis," Jerrod laughed. "Well, I might as well tell you. I do have business here in town. I've decided to semi-retire. I'm coming home to Cambridge."

"Great news!" Dennis raised his glass. "Here's to you and semi-retirement."

"That's not all," Jerrod continued with a broad smile. "Keep this under your hat though. I'm bringing a division of Michaelson & Associates to Cambridge. We've purchased property north of town. We break ground next spring. In 2013, when the facility's completed, twenty-five hundred folks from Guernsey and the surrounding counties will have steady employment with great wages and excellent benefits. Meantime, we'll put lots of people to work constructing the place. We've kept it quiet for obvious reasons. The few who needed to know are sworn to secrecy. The announcement will be made on New Year's Eve."

Dennis stared at Jerrod in stunned silence. Jerrod grinned in amusement.

"You look like you've just swallowed a bug, Dennis. Are you okay?" The smiling feminine voice trailed just over Jerrod's left shoulder. Turning toward the source, he quickly rose to his feet, almost spilling his beer in his haste.

"Elise!" Jerrod's heart pounded in his ears as he asked, "What a nice surprise. Please, join us?"

"Jerrod? Is that you? Omigosh!" She gave him a delighted hug. "How long has it been?" Slipping gracefully into a chair, she asked, "Dennis, what's going on here?" Jerrod couldn't help but glance at her left hand. There was no ring.

After dinner, the three stood talking outside the restaurant. Jerrod offered Cash a cup of water and watched the dog lap it up.

"Let's walk up the block," Dennis suggested, looking at his watch. "You're in for a real treat, Jerrod. Not only has Cambridge had an extensive makeover this past summer, but in a few minutes something wonderful happens at the Courthouse that you've got to see to believe. The crowd's already gathering."

As they walked, Jerrod realized the shops were all still open. People milled about downtown like movie extras getting ready for the big scene. The Christmas spirit was almost tangible. In the short distance to the courthouse, he saw three tour buses. "What's going on here?" he asked quizzically.

Smiling broadly, all Dennis would say was "You'll see."

As they reached the corner of Wheeling and Southgate, the courthouse lit up, as if on cue, in vibrant holiday colors, the beginning of a dazzling holiday light display. Mesmerized, Jerrod gasped in disbelief as Christmas lights danced around the courthouse, matching the rhythm of familiar Christmas carols. People ooh'ed and aah'ed, spontaneously singing along as color and music brought the old courthouse to life. Holiday spirit lit faces young and old. Dennis chuckled, watching Jerrod's chin drop in amazement. "I knew you'd like it," he grinned. "Everyone does." His gaze returned to the colorful spectacle.

"Cambridge is finally coming of age, you could say," Elise elaborated, the lights twinkling merrily across her countenance. A lot of people have worked hard to make good things happen here. We're moving into the future, but without leaving the past behind. Your new business venture will be a big boost too. I'm glad you decided to come home, Jerrod." Her voice wavered. "We…I…have been waiting a long time."

Taking her hand in his, Jerrod replied huskily, "You waited, Elise, and I'm thankful for that. I think you and I can make 2012 a very good year."

Cash yipped in agreement.

Star of Wonder

"Hey, Jack. I thought I'd find you here. The 'star' is due in three minutes. Am I right?" Yuri Sonin gave a quick pat on his friend's shoulder as he stopped alongside, staring steeply upward at the eastern sky. The patio where the two men stood, convenient to their adjoining three-story dorm, was dark, silent, and windless. The cold—not much below freezing—wasn't bad for mid-November. Crystal-clear constellations stretched out before the two lone men—a bleached blanket of light over the black steppes of Asia. The view to the east from Russia's Baikonur Spaceport was always good at night, for no one lived on that side of the station. That's where the rockets fell.

"You got it! It's coming in at minus eight, three degrees north of Deneb, same altitude. Gonna vector right to left. Haven't caught a 'star' this good in three months!" Jack paused, watching his breath for a moment. "You got the time marker ready?"

Space Shuttle pilot Jack Wilson glanced briefly at Payload Specialist Sonin, then back toward the sky, careful not to lose his orientation in the heavens. Sonin and Wilson, friends and associates for more than a decade, shared a special passion for the skies and for the things that men put there. On this particular night, they hunted for one particular satellite—a special one that would, by reflecting sunlight from its mirror-like antenna panel, leap out of the inky darkness for just a few seconds, burning like a ball of phosphorous—a thousand times brighter than anything else in the sky—and then be gone. It was all a matter of mathematics, angular reflections, and the uncanny precision of orbits. It was geeky—even geeky by astronaut standards—but it was also beautiful and fulfilling when the heavens, earth, and an unseen sun tucked just below the horizon signaled "all's well with the world" in a burst of affirmative light.

"Yes, I'll give you the countdown," Yuri assured Jack. The men stood together silently for nearly two minutes. "Thirty seconds," called Yuri. "Fifteen, fourteen, thirteen, twelve, eleven, ten…" The end of the countdown, as usual, ticked off silently in each man's mind as eyes scanned for the first signs of brightening. On cue, Iridium satellite 47 "flared up" three degrees north of fixed star Deneb. Ten seconds later, it was gone.

"That was great!" commented Jack, relieved as much by the sheer beauty of the sight as by the fact that his faith in orbital mechanics had once again been affirmed. "I suppose you heard that I'm leaving next week."

"Yes. I wanted to talk with you about that. Is it true, what I heard? It's the end?" Yuri quizzed.

"Yes. I've had a good run. I'm not complaining. The Shuttle's gone, and they're taking volunteers to downsize the astronaut corps. I'd rather leave voluntarily than be told to go. They don't need the pilots anymore." With a slight catch in his voice, Jack continued, "You know, Jim and Orin are leaving too. I counted up and there are at least five of us leaving who never got to fly. At least I can still say that once I was an astronaut, just like there are people in the Navy who've never been on a ship."

"I'm sorry, friend. But you're still ordered to hang out with us Ruskies whenever we're in Houston. You're going to stay in Houston, aren't you?"

"I'm not sure. I never really planned for this." Jack looked back up at the stars. "Somehow, life just seems to take me where I need to go. I always wanted to be an astronaut, but most of it was luck—like accidentally sitting next to just the right colonel in charge of selections on a civilian flight to Cleveland. They'd thrown out my three other applications. If I hadn't decided to fly back for Dad's retirement party that day, none of this would have happened. No simulator training. No trips to Russia. No banquets and people asking for autographs even though I've never been more than twenty miles above this planet. So much of it is luck!"

"I know," Yuri sympathized. "It's like that for me, too. I wouldn't be here if that train I was on thirty years ago hadn't broken down on the way to Leningrad. Well, actually, it's St. Petersburg now."

"You know," Jack said, "I'm 49 now. In the back of my head, I'd always thought that was a magic number since it's seven times seven. What's luckier than that? I thought that back when I was a kid too. Lucky seven times lucky seven! Remember the Mercury Seven astronauts? John Glenn flew in Friendship Seven, and he was born in my hometown, Cambridge." Jack smiled. "It's a town in Ohio where these two interstates meet, and their numbers are 70 and 77. I always thought it was sort of special, that in the whole United States, the luckiest-looking spot on the road map was right there at my hometown."

Jack paused to let another breath turn into fog and disappear. "I don't know what to make of it, but not ten minutes after I e-mailed my resignation to the Astronaut Office, I was thinking how I was a washed-up astronaut at 'lucky' 49—trying not to feel sorry for myself—when this paper letter gets put on my desk. It's an invitation to talk to kids back at my hometown over Christmas—the one where the sevens meet. Kinda spooked me. I shouldn't think it means anything, but it feels like it does. It feels like the luck again."

"Maybe it is," assured Yuri. "I'm superstitious, too. We all are. We pretend we're not, but we all are."

"What's your superstition?" Jack inquired.

"A special candle. I light it for luck right before suiting up for a trip to the space station. Then I pack it in my gear. It's a candle my mother gave me when I was in school, for doing homework when the power went out. She named me after Yuri Gagarin, you know, our first cosmonaut. He had just flown, but I was born the week your first astronaut went into space, and that has something to do with the candle, too. Can you guess?"

"Sure," replied Jack, not missing a beat. "'Light this candle!' Alan Shepard told them to fire the rocket's engine and launch."

"Very good! You know your history. He was sick of waiting through the launch holds, laying on his back, waiting for hours to go. So he just said 'Light this candle,' and off he went. We don't really know what Gagarin said before his flight, because Pravda used to make up whatever it wanted to pretend someone said—probably something about the good of the proletariat. I think Shepard got it right. Just light the candle. That's why I light the candle and take it with me. I'll light it again for next month's trip, too."

"That's your third trip, Yuri, you lucky dog! What are you going to do when you run out of candle?" chided Jack.

"I should be so lucky. I'm getting older too. I don't burn it long, so I'm sure it will outlast my career. In fact, I got special permission to light it at the station this time, sort of as a pretend science test. Without gravity, the flame doesn't know which way is up; no convection currents. It burns bright for just an instant, using up the oxygen that's right around the wick, and then it goes out. I'll film it and put it on the Internet. Kids love that stuff."

"You have excellent taste in superstitions, Yuri. I like it. Say, it's getting cold. Let's head in." Jack turned toward the dormitory as Yuri did the same, walking calmly toward the rusted Khrushchev-era east wing door of the sleeping quarters. "The station's coming by in an hour—kind of low in the southwest. Wanna watch that too?"

"Well, thanks, but I've got to write a report on the testing I was doing today with the new experimental setup your NSF sent me. Something about fruit flies in zero gravity. All I know's they're not going to like it—the fruit flies, that is. The NSF will probably just be happy to hear how much the flies don't like it." Knowing an inside joke, they both laughed.

An hour later, Jack Wilson reemerged from the dorm, stationed himself at a far edge of the patio, checked his watch, and stared low into the northwest sky. A point of light began to rise, brighten, and head rapidly clockwise well above the horizon, passing just below the North Star. Hitting earth's shadow, the space station dimmed and vanished in mid-air. Jack checked his watch. Once again, a little light in the heavens had just confirmed that all's well with the world.

Six weeks later found Jack a civilian again, in the town of the lucky sevens where long, long ago he had grown up. He wondered how a washed-up astronaut would be received. John Glenn was a hard act to follow. Few in the town even realized that a second son of Guernsey County had joined the astronaut corps and made it ever so close to the threshold of space. He could tell great stories about his years as a liaison between NASA and the Russian space program. He could even speak Russian—badly. He had some great 'war stories' about Shuttle simulator emergencies he had handled well, and a few that he didn't handle quite so well—the difference being that no matter how badly one mangles a spaceship by simulator, you get to drive your car home that night.

Mom and Dad were gone now. None of the cousins lived within an hour's drive. And a largely pleasant but unproductive marriage had ended two years before, the victim of too little time together and too much devotion to work. Wondering what it was that had brought him back to Cambridge—his town of the lucky sevens—at age 49, Jack pondered who it was he had become. Where he would go from here?

Jack's connecting flights from Houston to Atlanta to Pittsburgh on the day before Christmas had gone off without a hitch, as did the rental car drive to Cambridge's Hampton Inn. Exploring the town he hadn't seen since the early '90s, Jack came to sit in the early evening on a bench on the courthouse square. The cold—not much below freezing—wasn't bad for late December. Glancing at the sky, he checked his watch. By great good fortune, a satellite flare was due.

On the bench next to Jack's sat an attractive woman, looking to be roughly a well-preserved forty years old. Blond and trim, her red coat and printed scarf bespoke the festive expectations of the season, but her eyes were lost in reverie. Recognizing what he thought must be a bewilderment similar to his own, Jack decided he might as well reach out with a bit of holiday cheer.

"Excuse me, ma'am, but there's a Christmas Star going to show up in about thirty seconds just above the Soldiers' Monument there."

"What?" The woman looked puzzled as she snapped back to the here and now, slightly concerned that a nut might be sitting on the next bench over.

"Really, ma'am, if you'll just look above the monument, it'll be there in about twenty seconds now. Thought you might like to see it. Fourteen, thirteen, twelve, eleven. Keep looking. I think it's there for you."

As the silent count reached zero, a burst of light high above Southgate Parkway was noticed by two sets of eyes among the dozens milling about the square. A tear rolled down the woman's cheek, and then another. Turning toward Jack, she mouthed the words she couldn't speak, "Thank you." Looking as if she'd seen a ghost, she rose from the bench, turned away, and scurried off towards Seventh Street. Wondering what the "Christmas Star" had meant to the forlorn stranger, Jack smiled. Lady-tears notwithstanding, he thought it meant something good. His cell phone rang.

"Hello."

"Hey, Jack, Merry Christmas! I got Mission Control to patch me through. I'm gonna light the candle now, in your honor."

"Yuri, you old dog! It's great to hear from you!!" crowed Jack with an ear-to-ear grin. "How's trip number three going?"

"Oh, good, but the food's no better."

"Say, Yuri, remember the town with the lucky sevens I was telling you about back at Baikonur the night of that satellite flare? Well, that's where I am now. I don't know why, but it seems like the place I'm supposed to be."

"No, you're supposed to be up here, Jack. At least someday. You know, John Glenn was out of the astronaut corps for thirty years when he got to fly again. Never say never."

"If that's the way it works out, fine. Hey, guess what's at that 'lucky' interstate crossing I was telling you about. Actually, don't guess. There's a huge white cross there, beautifully lit at night. You can see it for miles around. And on top of that, there's good food in town, and the courthouse plays Jingle Bells!" Jack laughed.

"Good food! You're in the right place, man!" Yuri joked.

"Hey, Yuri, don't let me hold up your 'science experiment.' Go ahead and light that candle. It's time."

The International Space Station was making its third pass of the day over North America when a weightless candle owned by a superstitious cosmonaut flared and self-extinguished. A faint point of light emerged, brightened, and rose low in the sky far north of the courthouse square, but no one saw it. The courthouse, it seemed, had erupted in lights of its own. As the clock struck seven, the Trans-Siberian Orchestra's frenetic rendition of "We Three Kings" blared out over loudspeakers. On a bench in the courthouse square, a washed-up astronaut sang along softly under his breath. All was right with the world. The heavens above could wait, he knew, but just maybe the tearful lady could not. "Star of wonder..." Jack mused. Stationed close by the cross of the lucky sevens, he knew, was where he belonged this night.

A Most Special Christmas

Nancy Clare Roberts had no idea when she left Cambridge in 1981 that it would be thirty years before she would once again stroll along Wheeling Avenue, peering into store windows and waving at friends.

Now here she was, still half a world away, thinking about going home.

The vintage Cessna that had taken her from Chuuk to Weno then to Palikir in Micronesia, needed a refurbishing, inside and out. Padding was bursting through the seat upholstery and the engine emitted frightening, sputtering sounds. The craft shuddered violently as it banked sharply into a blinding squall then descended toward the bumpy runway at the international airport at Palikir. Nancy had less than an hour to board the Quantas jet in the capital of the Federated States of Micronesia to begin a laborious journey to Columbus.

The letter from educators in Cambridge had added impetus to her decision to leave the tropics. She had no idea how she could be of help in the Southeastern Ohio Symposium for Global Travel, but somehow the invitation to participate was intriguing.

What could be better than visiting old friends and relatives in Cambridge and, at the same time, imparting knowledge she had acquired as a businesswoman in far-off places?

At least she was booked on a large plane to Guam. Nancy never fully trusted the little single-engine puddle-jumpers and leaky skiffs that had moved her from island to island since she arrived in the islands nearly twenty years ago. Helping her with her luggage, Miki, the pilot, grinned as she alighted unsteadily on the flooded tarmac. "See you after the new year, Miss Nancy."

"Probably not," she said, avoiding his eyes. "Thanks for all of your service over the years, Miki, but I won't be coming back."

"Miss Nancy," Miki protested. "You go to Ohio? Too much snow and cold there."

"Yes," she said. "But it's something to look forward to, a traditional holiday with people I haven't seen in years."

Christmas in Cambridge, she sighed as the jet took off into the noon downpour. Nancy took one last look at the world she was leaving behind—little brown people scurrying for cover, palm trees bending nearly double in the savage wind, and ten-foot white-capped waves crashing against the pristine beaches.

She eased her lanky frame into the seat and closed her eyes, assuring herself that leaving her job in Micronesia was the right decision. First stop, Guam, then a layover in Hawaii. It would not be an easy trip. Perhaps that's why she never made an effort to go home for Christmas. The temperature in equatorial Palikar was eighty-eight degrees. A quick glance at a weather site on her laptop told her it was nine degrees in Cambridge, blanketed beneath four inches of snow, with another four on the way.

She smiled. For the first time in years she would experience a white Christmas instead of a steamy, soggy holiday surrounded mostly by natives who didn't believe in Jesus Christ. Still, she was apprehensive. Perhaps author Tom Wolfe was right when he wrote, "you can never go home." The Cambridge area had always had a reputation for friendliness. Nancy hoped nothing had changed. She had family there that she hadn't seen in years.

Sometimes she was nagged by guilt and regret at not maintaining closer ties with her home community. But she had been a woman driven by energy, intelligence, a yen to see the world, and an innate curiosity as to how far she could go in a business dominated by men.

A business degree from The Ohio State University and a master's degree from Northwestern University prepared her for the job in the tropics. Earning a six-figure salary, she had turned several islands into international tourist attractions. She secured funding to build upscale, gated retirement communities for wealthy Europeans, Australians, Americans, and Japanese. It hadn't been easy.

During her tenure in the North and South Pacific, she had written three books on the lifestyle of the islanders, two of which hit bestseller lists. Occasional royalty checks still came in.

Nancy had a two-hour layover and a change in airlines at the A.B. Won Pat airport on Guam, a facility that had been upgraded many times since her last visit. As she casually cruised the airport shops and boutiques, men slyly appraised her. Taller than average and athletically lithe, she exuded the confidence of a professional woman. Her dark brown hair, sprinkled with a few silver strands, seemed to add character to her finely chiseled features. Despite the wrinkles in her ivory linen business suit, she drew approving glances from passing men. Nancy was aware since her early college days that she was a head-turner, something that helped in her career.

Now that she was actually heading home four days before Christmas, she felt a tingle of excitement. The Christmas music in all the boarding areas helped. It had been a while since she had heard deeply religious Christian music during the holidays. Malaysia was mostly Islamic, something that concerned Nancy in recent years. While she never felt threatened in her everyday work schedule, she did experience growing apprehension because she was single and never gave up her Western ways.

She had been up for nearly twenty-four hours in her journey from one end of the world to the other. Even if she could catch a few winks on the next leg of her transmigration, she looked forward to sleeping in a plush Hawaiian hotel before embarking for San Francisco.

Ah, San Francisco, isn't that where Tony Bennett lost his heart? An old Al Jolson song ran crazily through her brain.

California, here I come;
Right back where I started from.
Where bowers of flowers bloom in the spring.
Each morning at dawning birdies sing at everything.
A sun-kissed friend said, "Don't be late!"
That's why I can hardly wait.
Open up that golden gate, California, here I come.

"Oh my gosh," she muttered to herself. "I must be losing it." Not really. Extremely worn out and perhaps a bit giddy.

Millions of lights twinkled upward as the jet circled Honolulu International Airport. The highways were packed with vehicles, most of them locked in impossible traffic jams. There was no escaping the Christmas madness as thousands of travelers rushed to be someplace special for the holidays.

It was a madhouse inside the terminal as Nancy confirmed her flight to San Francisco the next morning. She was now on American soil, but somehow Hawaii didn't have the holiday feel that she knew awaited her in San Francisco. She was a bit self-conscious boarding the plane. Her fresh black suit with a crisp mint green shell was the right winter color, but both the pants and jacket were extremely lightweight and meant for the tropics. She'd spend some of her layover time in San Francisco buying the heavy winter clothing she'd need for winter in Ohio. *What will woolen pants and a heavy turtleneck sweater, along with a bulky ski jacket, feel like,* she wondered.

A short weather broadcast on Honolulu TV noted that most airports across the upper Midwest were snowed in. That included Chicago, Cleveland, Columbus, and Pittsburgh. Nancy refused to let the bad news get her down. She was more than halfway home, fantasizing about the big roasted turkey, candied sweet potatoes, oyster dressing, and pumpkin pie for Christmas dinner.

Then there were the gift exchanges. Nancy had one suitcase filled with attractive and expensive artifacts from the islands—things her family and friends had never seen before. Hopefully, the pieces would find a prominent place in their homes.

When the jet reached cruising altitude, the strains of a familiar Christmas song wafted through the cabin: *"...where treetops glisten and children listen to hear sleigh bells in the snow..."*

Despite the dark skies and leaden clouds, the Golden Gate Bridge was a welcome sight as the plane made a wide circle over the city by the bay on its final approach to San Francisco International. A two-hour layover and about six more hours and Nancy would be home. She'd already called Enterprise and reserved a car in Columbus to be held for a late arrival.

Norman's was a pricy, high-style women's store inside the airport. Nancy decided on a garish powder blue argyle sweater; dark blue woolen pin stripe slacks; a heavy, mostly white ski jacket that covered her hips; and low-heeled boots with a heavy tread. Now she was ready for Cambridge in December.

Opting to wait until she arrived in Columbus to call her sisters in Cambridge, Nancy tied into a Wendy's triple burger and fries as she waited to board the plane. She'd almost forgotten what a real hamburger tasted like.

There was no time to dally at Chicago's O'Hare Airport, where the runways were wet but clear. She found herself racing to catch her final connecting flight to Columbus. One more hour in the air and she'd be in the land of the Buckeyes. Boarding the plane, she felt like bursting into the Ohio State fight song:

Drive, drive on down that line, Men of the scarlet and gray.
You've got to do or die, You've gotta win this game today...

Music, always music. How can it stir so much emotion? Nancy smiled as someone's iPod began playing:

Jingle bell, jingle bell, jingle bell rock
Jingle bell swing and jingle bell ring
Snowin' and blowin' up bushels of fun
Now the jingle bell hop's begun.

Enormous piles of fresh snow lined the Columbus runway as the plane crept toward the tarmac. The pilot said it was midnight and four degrees at the airport, but the skies were clear until mid-morning. Amazingly, all four of her large suitcases were waiting on the baggage carousel. Before taking the short walk to the car rental office, she called her sister, Angie, in Cambridge.

"Oh my gosh," Angie screamed. "Where are you?"

"Columbus. I'm practically home, Sis. It's the wee small hours, but I can't wait to see you all."

"How long have you been traveling?"

"I have no idea. Jet lag does that to you," Nancy laughed. "Is everyone all right?"

"Yes. You'll meet them tomorrow after you get some sleep."

"Okay, my car's ready and I'm on my way," Nancy said excitedly.

"Things have been happening so fast around here, with bad weather and Christmas, I forgot to ask if you've heard from Zach Stephens," Angie asked cautiously.

Nancy felt the cell phone slipping from her hand. *Zach Stephens?* "No," was her guarded reply.

"He called today and said he hoped to see you soon. He's part of the symposium. He knew you were invited to participate also."

Zach Stephens! Nancy barely noticed the huge snow dikes and icy pavement as she maneuvered the rental car on unfamiliar freeways leaving the airport. Following signs marked "Wheeling," she assumed she was headed for Cambridge.

Zach Stephens. Practically the only boy she dated at Cambridge High School. The big man on campus. Straight A's and a promising future. He often spoke of his love for her, and she returned that love. After he finished med school they'd make a life together, he'd promised.

She remembered the "Dear Nancy" letter, sent his sophomore year at Michigan. "It's best we see other people. We're young and face challenges as we pursue our careers." Then something about "keeping in touch" and remaining "friends always."

After that, all she knew was that Zach graduated medical school and was working at Johns Hopkins. She had brief relationships with a petroleum engineer from Tulsa who was working in Micronesia and an Australian marine biologist. Nice guys. Nothing more. Funny, smart, but little chemistry.

Lunch the following day with her sisters, Angie and Connie, along with their husbands and six children, was sheer bedlam. It was a combination of tears, giggles, hugs, and memories. The family was ecstatic with Nancy's Polynesian gifts.

At four o'clock, Angie and her husband took Nancy on a tour of Cambridge. Goodness, how the town sparkled in festive holiday finery. The downtown area was alive with beautiful twinkling store windows, mannequins from the Dickens era that lined Wheeling Avenue, and colorful streetlights.

"Somebody's been busy," Nancy remarked. "It's not like it was in the Seventies. And where did all this traffic come from? They used to roll up the sidewalks at sundown," she laughed.

"The town has worked hard to preserve what we have and to make some exciting plans for the years to come," Angie said proudly. "And we have a special surprise for you at six-thirty."

"And that would be...?"

"Our courthouse. Notice the buses lining the streets? They're filled with visitors who have traveled a long way to see our courthouse. The crowd gets larger every year," Angie smiled.

"Oh my gosh! Look at that!" Nancy cried out.

Suddenly, in the gathering darkness, with crystal-like snowflakes swirling in the air, the entire courthouse square came alive with flashing lights and techno music. Several hundred onlookers cheered and clapped at the gorgeous Christmas display. Traffic came to a standstill.

Nancy was stunned. "Absolutely breathtaking," she said softly. "I've been around the world for many Christmases, but I had to return to Cambridge to find the true beauty of the season."

"Are you crying?" Angie asked gently.

"Maybe just a little," Nancy sniffed, wiping her eyes. "I know it's cold as all get out, but let's mingle with the crowd."

Oh, come all ye faithful,
Joyful and triumphant
Oh, come ye, oh, come ye
To Bethlehem.

The spectacle continued. Children squealed in delight while locals and visitors mingled to share the fellowship of the season. The lump in Nancy's throat wouldn't go away. For the first time in her life, "home for the holidays" had real meaning.

She turned slowly when Angie called out, "Nancy! Do you remember this guy?" Angie giggled, allowing her arm to entwine with the tall man in a heavy jacket and a blue and white Bobcat stocking cap. "He says he knows you."

Nancy's lips moved but no sound came out. She stuttered like a giddy schoolgirl, "Zach Stephens..." Her voice trailed off. Then she muttered something silly like, "Oh my…"

There was no mistaking the dancing eyes and quick smile when Zach hugged her. Then, gently holding her at arm's length, he said, "Since my divorce in ninety, I've worked in hospitals in South America and with Doctors without Borders on the Ivory Coast. How long are you going to stay in Cambridge?"

"Maybe forever," Nancy whispered, kissing his cheek lightly.

"Me too," Zach grinned.

A Timely Invitation

Sergeant Roy Fitzgerald stretched out on his cot, thoughtfully staring at the ceiling and wondering, *What's next?* Twenty-five years old and a rifleman in the U.S. Army, Roy had arrived in the states near the end of the war in Europe after several weeks in a military hospital in Italy due to a serious leg wound.

Tall and thin, with haunting blue eyes and thick black hair, Roy came from a long line of Irish-American soldiers, his father had served in WWI in France, his grandfather a victim of one of the rebellions in Ireland. But Roy wasn't a warrior. A gentle, peace loving man, he joined the Army a few months after WWII broke out; just a patriotic man who wanted to serve his country.

By temperament, talent, education, and experience, he was an artist and sculptor. A graduate of Columbus College of Art and Design, he'd just started his career as a designer for a pottery company in Virginia when the Japanese attacked Pearl Harbor.

Roy turned to look at the young soldier in the next bed. Having lost an arm in a grenade explosion, the man was in a deep depression. Wherever Roy looked, he saw despair. Many of these men had broken spirits as well as broken bodies.

Studying the patients in this ward, he saw young men, boys really, many in worse shape than he. *At least I still have my hands and my ability. Finding a job in my field may be a problem but I have plenty of time to think about that. For now, I'll sweat out the healing process and get ready for some intense rehab.*

His thoughts turned to his girlfriend and the "Dear John" letter he had received at the hospital in Italy. *I guess the thought of spending the rest of her life with a potential cripple was more than she could take. Well, I can't say I blame her, but it hurts.*

Roy was a patient at Fletcher General, a Fifth Service Command orthopedic hospital in Cambridge, Ohio. It had been a long war but the allies were once again victorious and the troops were returning to the states, if not their homes. Now it was Christmas time. Every ward was gaily decorated, and the cafeterias, PX, auditorium, even the gym.

Roy lucked out when he was sent to Cambridge. He was from Columbus and his folks could visit often. They, along with his younger sister, would be here Christmas morning and he was anxious to spend the day with them.

Faintly, singing voices crept into his thoughts. Rising from his bed and reaching for his crutches, he slowly joined other G.I.'s making their way to the corridor door. Looking in the direction of the music, Roy could see no one. "Must be a radio," he said, returning to his bed. But the voices got stronger and he recognized the strains of 'Oh, Little Town of Bethlehem.' *Oh, how sweet, how familiar.* He hadn't heard the carol for so long, but now he remembered every word, every note.

Returning to the doorway, he could see a group of carolers in the distance, their voices becoming stronger as they approached his ward. It was a mixed ensemble from Cambridge High School, led by a small lady wearing a very serious dark suit and sensible shoes. A tight, short perm framed her face and horn-rimmed glasses perched on her nose. The only sign of the holiday was a bejeweled Christmas tree broach pinned to her lapel. She carried a notebook of music in one hand and clutched a purse with the other. At the carol's last refrain, the lady piped a new key and the group joyously broke into 'Oh, Come All Ye Faithful.'

Soon the doorways to each ward were crowded with young, lonely, broken G.I.'s., back after months, sometimes years, in war-torn countries. They watched with tearstained faces as they stood, leaned, or sat, mesmerized by the familiar sounds.

As the last strains faded, a weak voice asked, "Could you please favor us with 'Oh, Holy Night,' Ma'am?"

"I'm sorry, soldier," answered the lady. "That carol is always done with accompaniment."

Seeing disappointment in Sgt. Roy Fitzgerald's eyes, one of the young ladies in the group said, "Oh please, Miss Lloyd, can't we try it anyway? I'm sure we could do it."

Reluctantly piping the key of B flat, the director led the mixed chorus of young voices in a heartfelt rendition of the beautiful carol. As the last notes faded, all was quiet for a few moments, followed by applause peppered with soft sounds of sobbing as the group quietly progressed down the hall.

The next day, Roy made his way to the PX, where visiting civilians milled about among the soldiers. He carried his purchases to the register, where he recognized the cashier. It was the young girl who had convinced the music director to sing 'Oh, Holy Night' a cappella. Waiting his turn, he studied her. *Beautiful girl, really quite striking. What's she's doing here?* When Roy's turn came, she smiled, recognizing him.

"Well, hello, again," she offered. "Nice to see you. Did you find everything you need?"

Grinning, Roy replied, "I sure did and I'm very glad to see you. What are you doing here today?"

"I'm with the volunteers who help wherever we're needed. Here at the PX or distributing magazines, candy, and notions to the wards…that kind of thing. With the holidays and a shortage of help, I'm everywhere. Some of the GI's have gone home for a few days, but I see you aren't one of them. I'm so sorry."

"It's okay. I'm from Columbus. My family will be here Christmas Day. Don't suppose you'll be here then?" Roy asked slowly.

"Actually, I will be for three hours in the afternoon. If you have time, why don't you drop by? I'd like to meet your family."

"We'll make time," he grinned. "See you then, and Merry Christmas."

Picking up his change, Roy expertly maneuvered his crutches, heading for the door. Suddenly he stopped, turned back, and called to the girl. "I don't know your name," he declared.

"Colleen McNeil," she answered. "And you are…?"

"Roy. Roy Fitzgerald. Goodbye for now, Colleen."

"Goodbye, Roy."

"Colleen McNeil," he softly repeated. "Irish, of course."

As Roy exited the PX, he whistled 'Joy to the World.'

Christmas Day, and Coleen McNeil's schedule had been changed. She'd had to report in early and wondered if she'd see Roy Fitzgerald, if he even came by. With her shift over, she'd be going home soon. As she prepared to leave, the Fitzgerald family entered the PX. Ray, wearing a big grin, quickly approached her.

"Ah, Colleen. Merry Christmas. Just coming to work?"

"No, just leaving," she replied. "My hours were changed. I'm glad I didn't miss you."

"Please," invited Ray, "I'd like you to meet my family."

Patrick and Ellen Fitzgerald and young Janie chatted with Colleen as Roy looked on, his admiration growing as he studied the charming girl. Dainty, with long hair and blue eyes a guy could drown in, she was very animated as she asked the group if they'd had their Christmas dinner. "No," Ellen replied. "We are going there now."

"Why don't you come home with me?" she asked. "My folks have open house on Christmas Day, a custom they began when the hospital opened. There'll be games, caroling, good cheer, and plenty of food." Seeing the grin on Ray's face, the Fitzgerald's quickly accepted the gracious invitation.

Roy Fitzgerald and Colleen McNeil were married the next Christmas Eve at St. Benedict Church among family and friends.

On leaving the hospital a few months earlier, Roy had secured a position at Universal Pottery, doing what he loved to do. His new father-in-law, an executive there, was instrumental in getting him an interview, but Roy was hired on his own merits, as his talents and engaging personality were very impressive. Colleen McNeil Fitzgerald was by then attending the Cambridge Business College and working part-time for a local law firm.

Life was good for the Fitzgerald's in 1949, when they welcomed their first child, Roy Scott Jr., known to the family as Scotty. He was followed by two more boys and finally twin girls. The Fitzgerald kids faithfully attended St. Benedict schools and church, where Scotty was an attentive student with a great thirst for knowledge. His mother frequently admonished him, calling, "Scotty, will you please get your nose out of that book and help your brothers with their homework?"

On graduating high school, Scotty and later his brothers were accepted at Notre Dame College, where Scotty majored in education and his brothers majored in football and girls.

Notre Dame. That's where Scotty met and married sweet Rosalie Kinnen. Scotty loved Rosalie and he loved teaching. He had done his student teaching at a church school and at graduation secured a position at a Chicago high school. Later, working nights on his Master's, he taught at the University of Chicago. Sadly, Scotty and Rosalie were never blessed with children but felt like parents to his students in the coming years.

He lost his beloved Rosalie to a brave, but losing, battle with cancer. Having received tenure, Scotty decided to visit Africa, where he had a growing interest in the schools. He was teaching in a small, remote school in the Congo when he received an invitation to attend a symposium in his hometown in December.

Eagerly, he accepted the invitation. It had been a couple years since he had visited his aging mother, his father having died several years ago. Now he was on his way home...home for Christmas. His brothers, sisters, and their families would be there too. As his plane neared Port Columbus he was visibly anxious.

Sister Anne Roy, Scotty's sister, was a nun. She would be there to meet him. She too was a teacher and head of St. Benedict schools. His other sister, Mary, was mother of four. She and her husband would arrive from Canton. His brothers had joined the business world and lived with their families in New York City.

As Anne Roy, expertly maneuvering the aging van through traffic, neared Cambridge, she chatted on about what her brother was about to see. "You won't know the place, Scotty. Never has Cambridge been so beautiful, not even in the fall."

"What's going on?" he asked.

"I don't have words to describe it," she answered. "I don't think anyone could. You'll have to see for yourself."

Scotty was awestruck as the van made its way up Southgate Parkway. He noted figures of colorfully dressed Victorian characters. *Straight out of Dickens*, he thought in wonder.

Anne Roy found a parking place and, urging him to follow her, quickly jumped from the van. As they neared the Guernsey County courthouse, he saw the dancing lights; thousands of colored lights covering the building. And there on the corner in front of him was his family, wearing bright smiles. With arms outstretched, they embraced him just as the melancholy sounds of the holiday favorite, 'I'll Be Home for Christmas,' filled the air. *Not in my dreams this time,* thought Scotty, *no, not in my dreams. This time it's for real.*

HOME FOR CHRISTMAS

Staring at the walls of the NCO barracks, Chief Master Sergeant Todd Brooks pondered over the last thirty years of his life. Tall and thin with silver-grey hair, the chief had been all over the world, through three wars, two deployments, and three failed marriages.

Now he was back where it all began, living in the barracks. *Well,* he thought, *I can hack this for a few months till my time is up. At least there are no more open bay barracks with all your stuff crammed in a metal foot locker. Whoever would have thought there would be cable TV in the barracks?*

Todd fumbled in his pocket for his glasses as he sorted through a week's worth of mail. Buried among all the junk mail was a letter in the now all too familiar handwriting of his mother. As he opened it, a small card with a religious icon on the front, detailing the recent death of his Uncle Joe, fell out. Mom's letters always started the same and ended with a prayer for his safety.

Dear Todd, hope this letter finds you in good health and safe. We are all OK; just getting older. But here the letter was different from the usual ones. Her handwriting was a little shaky; it went on. *Dad and I have decided to sell the farm and move into town. Actually, the town has moved to us since they built the new Walmart where the old Moore house used to be.* His mother had an endearing way of reflecting on the past to keep him posted on current events. *It's just too big and too much for us to keep up anymore. It was a hard decision to make with all you kids being raised here. We always hoped one of you would want this place. To get to the point, we have invited everyone back for one last Christmas at home. Hope you can make it. It's been a long time since you have been here. It would mean so much to us to have everyone together one last time. As always, Mom.* There was a P.S. *I have a very important matter to discuss with you when you get home.*

Todd put his hands behind his head as he lay back, allowing his mind to drift back to when he was a kid and life was a lot simpler. Christmas was the best time of the year. His family lived next door to Grandma and Grandpa, who had a big family. Everyone came home for Christmas back then. A few days before Christmas, people would drift in and out of the house wishing everyone a Merry Christmas and a prosperous New Year.

It was a ritual that didn't change until his senior year in high school. That was when his older brother Stan left for pilot training in the Air Force. His mother still set a plate at the table for him even though it was impossible for him to come home.

I remember it well, Todd thought. *There would be two empty spaces the next year, when I joined up. Little did I know that one of those places would soon be empty forever. Maybe one last time,* he thought, closing his eyes. M*aybe one last time.*

After a restless night and a quick shower and shave, he headed for the orderly room. "Is the old man in?" he asked the clerk.

"You can go in, Chief; he's having his morning coffee."

Todd first served under Colonel David in Vietnam, then in the first Gulf War, and more recently in Iraq. They were old friends.

Knocking before he entered, Todd was surprised to see him pouring two cups of coffee. Colonel David motioned for him to take a seat. "I think you drink it black, don't you, Todd?"

"That will be fine, Sir."

"What can I do for you? I heard you moved back into the barracks. How is that going?"

"It's changed a lot in the last thirty years, but it will work until I decide what to do."

"If you decide to stay in, Todd, I could arrange a desk job for you."

"What I would like is a leave. I want to go home for Christmas. It's been a long time since the family has been together for the holidays."

"Where might home be, Todd?"

"Ohio, Sir. Actually southeastern Ohio, a little town called Cambridge."

"Have you made any arrangements?"

"No, Sir. I just decided last night."

"There is a courier flight going to Wright-Patterson in Dayton tomorrow morning. I know the colonel at Base Ops. I could arrange a seat for you."

"That would be great, Sir."

The plane was practically empty, with the exception of a row of cargo in the middle aisle. Todd strapped himself in for the long flight, then asked a young sergeant sitting next to him to wake him when they got to Dayton. The low monotonous whine of the engines soon lulled Todd to sleep. It seemed like only a few minutes when the jar of the landing woke him. Stepping out onto the freezing tarmac, he pulled his coat collar up around his neck, suddenly remembering what Ohio winters were like.

"Need a ride, Chief?" the pilot asked as they walked from the hangar. "This is my home base. I'm off duty now, heading for Trotwood and a nice, home-cooked meal."

"Could you drop me off at the bus depot?"

"Not a problem, Sir. Jump in."

The bus depot was crowded with Christmas travelers. Todd took a seat in the back. As the bus headed east on I-70, he gazed out the frosty window at the snow-covered farms. Suddenly, he realized he actually missed this. *It's peaceful,* he thought. *Nature's way of telling us to rest.*

The bus stop in Cambridge was a big surprise; there was no longer a terminal on Wheeling Avenue. Passengers were dropped off at a service station at the edge of town. Todd called his mom from a nearby pay phone as he lit a cigarette. *Dad and I used to hunt rabbits here when I was a kid,* he thought. *This was pretty much a wetland.*

Startled from his daydreaming by the honk of a horn, Todd turned to see his Dad's Ford pickup truck pull up beside him. As he opened the door, he tossed his duffle bag in the truck bed. "You look great, Mom," he said, giving her a quick kiss on the cheek. "How do you feel? I can't believe you're still driving this old truck. I thought Dad would come."

"Your father doesn't drive anymore…it's his eyes. I dropped him off at Theo's. He's having coffee with his friends." It was then Todd noticed the cane tucked in beside his mom. Driving down Southgate Parkway, he was amazed at all the businesses that had sprung up there.

"Who would have thought all this would be here," Todd remarked. "This was a swamp."

"There have been lots of changes since you left, Son. We have a new high school north of town, several banks and drugstores, and the downtown has been completely renovated. Cambridge goes all-out for Christmas. We'll drive you uptown tonight so you can see the lights. Sadly, most of the factories have moved overseas."

"Is the spark plug factory still there?" Todd asked, his voice trailing off.

"Yes, and your brother Stan would be alive today if he would have stayed there. He could have been retired by now. I never understood why he had to join the Air Force…now he's MIA somewhere in that God-forsaken country," she said, sobbing.

Todd reached over to touch her shoulder. "Stan always wanted to fly, Mom. It was all he ever talked about. Remember all the model airplanes he had in our room?"

"I know, Todd, I know…it's what makes selling the house so difficult. My memories of him are all I have left. Soon that will be gone too." As she pulled to the side of the snow-covered road to wipe her eyes, Todd hugged her.

Their house was at the end of a long driveway. Todd noticed the house was painted beige. "How did you convince Dad to paint it beige? I thought white was the only color he knew."

"That's a long story," his mother replied. "I'll pick him up in a minute, but first we need to talk."

With the exception of some new curtains, everything was the same in his old room as it was when he and Stan shared it. Todd sat on edge of the bed. His mother followed him shortly, carrying a letter. "I received this a few weeks back. It's from a man who claims to be Stan's son. His name is Stan Nugent, and he wants to come for a visit. He asked about you, Todd!"

"Stan Nugent!" Todd exclaimed, grabbing the letter from his mother. Todd's hands shook as he read the letter. He bent over, burying his face in the palm of his hands as the letter fell to the floor.

"He's alive," Todd murmured, looking up. "I can't believe he's alive and he's here in America." Retrieving the letter, Todd slowly read aloud the details of the man's miraculous escape from Vietnam. A startled look crossed his mother's face.

"You knew about this," his mother exclaimed. "Why didn't you tell us? How could you do this to us?"

"Sit down, Mom. Let me explain," Todd began. "Stan and Li were very much in love. She was a kindergarten teacher at the American mission in Saigon. It was love at first sight. But it was illegal for Americans to marry Vietnamese. Finally, a Catholic priest secretly married them. A year later, Stan Jr. was born. Stan planned to get out of the Air Force when his tour was up and he had returned home. Then he'd send for them. Things just got bad after that. First, Stan's plane went missing over Laos. It turned into chaos when we started withdrawing. I spent two days at the American Embassy trying to get a passport for them. Like I said, it was total chaos. The last time I saw them, they were on a bus trying to get to Thailand. I never heard from them again."

"Why did Stan keep this a secret from us?"

"Well, seeing Dad's dislike for Orientals, Stan wanted to tell him in person."

"I better get your father. He doesn't know about this."

Later that evening as they sat down for dinner, Todd noticed the empty plate his mom still set for Stan. Toward the end of the meal, as she cleared the table, she looked at her husband. "Dad, Todd has something to tell you," she said quietly.

Todd pulled a pack of Camels from his shirt pocket. Lighting one, he pushed back from the table as he exhaled a cloud of blue-grey smoke. Over the next hour, several cigarettes, and another pot of coffee, Todd told his folks all he knew about Stan and Li.

"Well, now I know why he wanted to stay over there," his father said as he looked out the window.

"You need to read this, Dad," his wife said, handing him the letter. "This came a few weeks ago. I didn't know what to do, so I wrote to Todd. He thinks it could be...well...what do you think?"

After reading the letter, Todd's father looked at him. "Could this be true? Could he be alive?" he asked thoughtfully.

"I think so. The boy has those funny little fingernails like Stan and Mom. It appears Li told him a lot about his father."

"The letter says he's going to Ohio State," the old man remarked. "If that's his phone number, I think it's time we give him a call."

Todd picked up the phone and walked into the living room. A few minutes later, he returned. "He'll be here Sunday for dinner," he announced to his surprised parents.

Sunday arrived with a flurry of activity. Todd put his arms around his mom as they looked down the long driveway. "It will be OK, Mom. Slow down. If he's like Stan, he won't arrive with a lot of high expectations."

A black Ford Mustang turned off the main road and parked next to the mailbox. A tall, lanky man with Asian features emerged. Hesitantly, he slung a bag over his shoulder and walked to the front door. He had short coal-black hair, wore wire rim glasses, and walked with a slow, deliberate gait.

"Oh, my God," Todd's mom shouted, clutching Todd's arm. "He walks like Stan, and he's driving a Mustang! Stan had one too."

After introductions and some pleasantries, the lad told his story.

"When the Communists took over, they were hard on everyone who associated with the Americans. We were sent to a re-education camp. Mom changed our name back to Nugent, hoping we wouldn't stand out. We lived there, working in the rice patties until I was sixteen. Then I was drafted into the Army. That was the last time I saw Mom. When we were on maneuvers next to the Thailand border, I defected. After years of working odd jobs, I applied for a visa for Vietnamese children who had American fathers. I came to Ohio because Mom said that was where Dad was from. I Googled your name and finally got the nerve to write the letter," the boy said.

Opening his bag, he spilled the contents on the coffee table. There before them lay Stan's high school ring, his graduation watch, and some old photos and letters. "Mom gave me these the last time I saw her," Stan said.

Everyone in the room burst into tears. Trying to compose herself, Todd's mom finally stood up. "Dinner is ready. Stan, you sit next to Todd. Your Uncle Todd, that is."

For the next hour, they chatted over bygone years. Suddenly Stan blurted, "Look, Mrs. Brooks, you have fingernails like mine."

Todd's mom reached over and squeezed his hand. "Isn't it about time you started calling us 'Grandma' and 'Grandpa'?"

"Finally," Stan shouted, tears streaming down his cheeks. "I've found my home, in Cambridge, Ohio!"

"So have I," Todd nodded. "So have I."

Feel the Vibes

Who do you turn to when a child disappears and you haven't a clue? Sharon Michelle, world famous psychic detective, could be the best answer. This psychic, who resembles your favorite grandmother, has found lost children in countries all over the world for forty years.

Take the case of bonny Glenda McDougal, who wandered off through the woods with Sean, her teddy bear. As this perky young lass skipped across the iron latticed bridge back in the woods, her soft, cuddly bear slipped from her hand, falling into the bubbling stream below. Glenda leaned through the railing to reach her little friend, but couldn't stretch quite that far and instead got stuck between the rails.

When Glenda didn't arrive home for supper, her mathair *(mother)* started calling, "Glenda, Glenda, where are you? It's time to eat." No one answered.

Since she definitely was "Daddy's little girl," Athair *(Father)* McDougal got busy calling the police, who checked all the obvious places around the little town of Larkhall, Scotland. No one remembered seeing the young girl or her teddy bear that afternoon.

How could they find her? The McDougal's couldn't sleep that night and police said they would have to wait until morning to continue the search. Predictions of heavy rain and thunderstorms the following day put Mathair McDougal in a panic. She decided to call the world famous psychic detective, Sharon Michelle, to see if she could help them locate her precious daughter.

Sharon happened to be in London, so arrived at the McDougal home quickly by plane. There, she asked for a toy that Glenda frequently held. Mathair McDougal handed the clairvoyant a big pink bunny that Glenda cuddled at night. Sharon Michelle touched and smelled the bunny to feel the energy of the little girl.

After several minutes, she told Glenda's parents, "I see your daughter on a bridge deep in the woods. The rails keep her body wedged tightly. Appears she is reaching for something over the side of the bridge."

"That might be the little bridge over Bubbling Brook where our cows drink," remarked an excited Athair McDougal. "Let's head down there and see what we can find. She might be there."

They rescued Glenda and Sean shortly and brought them home for some Tender Loving Care...and warm scones topped with butter and strawberry jam.

Rescues like these made Sharon Michelle famous and frequently sought after all over the world. Psychic detectives seem to appear at the right place at the right time when people have the courage to use unconventional means to locate someone missing. Most local police departments resist using psychics and often frown on their interference. But when parents get to the end of their rope, they will try almost anything. And who can complain if it really works?

One morning a letter arrived, asking the world renowned detective to attend the Symposium for Global Travel in Cambridge, Ohio, at Christmastime. *That might work out just fine since I'm finished with the investigation here at The Woodlands in Texas. Could be a relaxing drive to beautiful Ohio. Perhaps I'll have time to find the old farm where I grew up and even locate my brother, Walter.*

Even psychics need a break from all the meditation involved, so Sharon Michelle decided to head back home to Doughty Hollow, near Boden, Ohio. Christmastime would be the perfect chance to check on her family. She hadn't been to the old home place since her teenage years, but had many fond memories. At that time, she was called Sherry by her family and friends. Her psychic ability surfaced there as a child when her dog didn't come home one evening.

That long ago night, she called and looked everywhere for her collie, Pal. Her brother and sister assisted her, but Pal could not be found. Sherry cried herself to sleep that night holding Pal's favorite toy, an old rubber bone. Her dreams showed Pal in an old abandoned coal mine where several boards had fallen down to trap him.

Next morning she told her brother, Walter, about her dream. Walter said, "That could be the old mine over on the Smith place. Let's go check it out."

When they got close, Sherry whispered, "Listen." She could hear Pal's weak barks coming from deep in the hillside. Walter and Sherry crawled back in the mine and, sure enough, Pal's head peeked out under fallen ceiling rafters. He barked happily when he saw them!

Sharon Michelle was known all over the world but her family never could understand her abilities. They just said it was by chance that she found Pal that day and were skeptic of all psychics. So after her parents died, she had lost contact with her brother and sister.

Wonder if the old farm house is still there? Wonder if Walter still lives anywhere around? The closer she got to Cambridge, the more apprehensive she became. When she left the area as a teenager to travel the world as part of the Peace Corps, schoolmates considered her eccentric. Would she be accepted now?

Upon arrival, she decided to stay on Southgate Parkway at

one of the motels, but wondered if that place that sold pizzaburgers, The Mecca, was still in business. She remembered them well from high school years and thought that would be a great way to start off her return visit. So she headed up towards the courthouse and couldn't believe her eyes. The courthouse sparkled with moving lights and she could hear Christmas music playing. Wow! This spectacular light show stopped cars and buses along the streets, and the spirit of Christmas could be felt in the air.

As she turned down Wheeling Avenue, she also noticed all the Victorian figures along the street. Cambridge had really changed. Tomorrow, she would have to take a walk and view the figures more closely. But, for now, her hunger guided her to that pizzaburger restaurant and eased when she saw the sign: 'Mr. Lee's, Home of the Pizzaburger.' Yum!

"Please give me a pizzaburger and an order of your delicious onion rings," said Sharon Michelle, licking her lips in anticipation. "I haven't been in Cambridge for many years and hope they taste as good as I remember."

"I think your taste buds will get a treat as they haven't changed much," said Mr. Lee, who had owned the Mecca years ago. "It will be ready in a few minutes. Would you like to read the Jeffersonian while you wait, and catch up on local news?"

Glancing at the newspaper, the front page headline told the story of a boy, Craig Brunski, missing from his home right here in town since last night. *Oh, my! It is wintertime out there and that poor boy must be very cold,* thought Sharon. *Why it's so cold a polar bear would be knockin' at the door to come in.* The Jeffersonian reported the last time Craig was seen, he was riding his bicycle with his dog, Shaggy, following him.

Wonder if I might be able to help, thought the psychic lady. *Perhaps someone here at the restaurant could tell me where the boy lives and I could talk to his parents.*

"Is there any chance I could get that order to go? Something urgent has come up."

"Certainly, it'll be ready in a minute."

"I noticed this story about the lost boy. Would you happen to know where he lives? I'd like to talk to his parents."

"Oh yes," said Ralph, the busy manager. "I'll draw directions for you. They're actually customers here, and I know they're as anxious as a turkey at Thanksgiving about the boy's disappearance."

So off Sharon Michelle went with her pizzaburger, eating while she drove to the Brunski house. When she arrived, she thought, *Now, how am I going to introduce myself to these strangers? Should I tell them I'm a psychic detective? How will they react?* All these questions filled her mind, but she knew she had to help.

Up to the door she went and gently knocked. Mrs. Brunski answered the door quickly, but a disappointed look replaced her hopeful countenance when she saw a stranger at the door. Probably hoped that the police had found Craig and Shaggy and were bringing them home. But instead, outside her door stood an older lady with long auburn hair dressed in jeans and parka.

"Hello, my name is Sharon Michelle and I just saw the story in the paper about your son. Often, I help find lost children by psychic sensations. Would you mind if I tried to help?"

"Well, that sounds strange to me, but at this point I am so frightened that I will try anything. Craig's been gone now for over a day and the police haven't been able to help us. How can you help?"

"First thing I need," insisted Sharon Michelle, "is something he would either wear often or carry in his pocket."

"Well," thought his mother, "Let me see if I can find his favorite Ohio State tee shirt. He sleeps in it a lot, so it might work."

While Mrs. Brunski went to the bedroom to check for the shirt, Sharon Michelle sat down in a chair in the living room to relax so she could concentrate better. Mr. Brunski, nervously walking the room in circles, almost made her dizzy.

The Ohio State shirt did indeed give off vibes of Craig. When Sharon Michelle closed her eyes, a flash passed through her mind and she described Craig to his parents.

"I see a boy with very short reddish blond hair, wearing a dark blue winter jacket with a hood. He feels panicky but is not severely injured."

"Sounds like Craig! C-c-can you tell where he is?" pleaded an excited Mrs. Brunski.

After a deep breath, Sharon Michelle closed her eyes waiting for another flash. In a dreamy voice, she told them, "I see an empty house and some of the numbers on it are 4, 7, and 8. There are woods nearby. He appears to be trapped by something."

The only woods the mother could recall nearby grew on the edge of town near the park. Was there an empty house there? "Come on, let's take a ride that direction," said Mr. Brunski, a man of few words. They all piled in his SUV and off they flew down the street.

All at once they spotted the house number of 1478 and the house was indeed dark, with a For Sale sign in the front yard. Frantically, they parked the SUV and walked all around the house. At the back stairs, they found Craig's bicycle. Mr. Brunski discovered a door that was partly open, so they cautiously looked inside.

What did they see? Craig had fallen through the floor and couldn't get out. Shaggy stayed by his side, licking his face. As quickly as possible, they removed a few rotted boards that had given way and pulled Craig free.

"We're so glad you're OK," said his mom and dad, with tears in their eyes as they hugged him. "We worried about you and looked all night long. Why did you come in this house?"

"Well, I know I probably shouldn't have come in the door but Shaggy ran inside and I went after him," stammered a frightened Craig. "Thanks for getting me out of there."

"You better thank Sharon Michelle," urged his mom. "Without her, we would never have found you."

Everyone shivered in the cold night air. They quickly piled into the warm SUV to head back to the Brunski's house. "Wait until I tell Uncle Walter about this!" exclaimed Craig. "He won't believe it,"

"Wait a minute," questioned Sharon Michelle. "Where does your Uncle Walter live?"

"He lives out in Doughty Hollow," replied Mrs. Brunski.

"Doughty Hollow! Could that be Walter Charleston?"

"Why, yes! He is my mother's brother."

"This can't be! He is my brother, too," cried out Sharon Michelle. "That would make you my niece! Is your name Marilyn?"

"Wow, it is definitely a small world. Hard to imagine that my own aunt is the psychic detective who rescued my little boy. It has been so long since you left; I never expected you to show up just when we needed you most."

"Well, I think it's time for a family celebration. Let's all go downtown and watch the courthouse light show."

"Just a minute. Before we go," shouted Marilyn as she ran up the steps excitedly, "I need to get something special." When she returned, she carried a yellowed sheet of paper in her hand.

"Do you remember drawing this about fifty years ago? My mother gave me this picture and said her sister told her that someday our courthouse would look like this. Let's go see how your psychic touch was working years ago."

On the courthouse square, they were all surprised at how accurately Sharon Michelle had seen this image of the future when she was a child. The mind is indeed a mystery. She had drawn the scenes in the courthouse windows, decorations on the trees in front, and all in beautiful colors.

"Welcome home, Aunt Sherry," said Marilyn. "Thanks for the great family celebration tonight, and I know Walter will be anxious to see you."

Tomorrow, she would be paying a visit to Doughty Hollow to surprise Walter. Certainly felt lucky, or perhaps it was a psychic connection, that she happened to come back to Cambridge when she did...for many reasons.

INTO THE WIND

Alex Butterfield drove the rental car swiftly along U.S. 30 East on his way from Chicago to Ohio. He'd just endured a draining week at a deadly boring, but mandatory, chemical symposium. Now he was looking forward to seeing old friends in Cambridge. The short drive was just what he needed to unwind before he got there.

They'd be surprised to see him, a balding divorced man wearing tiny silver spectacles that stood up on his nose like a pigeon getting ready to take flight. He was no longer the muscular football player they'd voted "Most Likely to Succeed" in high school, but he had exceeded their expectations in more important areas. Indeed, he had succeeded so well that he could donate very generously to the progressive updating of Cambridge's downtown area. This trip home was a treat he'd been anticipating for many months, his first opportunity to see the changes, and especially the courthouse light show.

He'd been in and out of the country for the last three years, based in the San Fernando Valley of California, but regularly tromping around the temperate rain forests of Valdivia, Chile. An internationally respected chemist involved in Chilean cranberry product development, Alex had come to love the country of Chile and the fragrant strawberry scent of the beautiful pink-tinged cranberry blossoms. His research had resulted in identification of twenty-three pharmaceutical uses for the fruit and leaves of the handsome shrub.

As he sped along a desolate stretch of U.S. 30, Alex felt the car hydroplane over an icy patch. Instinctively, he let up on the gas, but the car didn't slow down; instead, it spun sideways, traveling along the frozen roadway for thirty long seconds. Alex watched in horrified fascination as the accident played out before his eyes in slow motion. The right side tires slipped off the edge of the pavement. His eyeglasses lifted from his nose and sailed through the air, coming to rest briefly in the back seat just as the car began to roll. The air bags deployed, pushing the breath out of his lungs, pinning him to his seat while momentum rolled the car three times. He felt like a rag doll in the muzzle of a Doberman pinscher, too numb with shock to feel the pain exploding in his gut. Finally, agonizingly, the car stopped, coming to rest passenger side down against an old walnut tree, which shuddered with the impact and promptly dropped a massive aging limb onto Alex's door. Alex threw up and passed out.

When he came to and the spinning in his head subsided sufficiently, Alex examined the twisted wreckage encasing him, amazed that he'd lived through the carnage. He giggled a little when he realized his feet were bare, shoes and socks literally blown off by the collision. Astounded at his good fortune, he extricated himself easily from behind the wheel and climbed out gingerly, a little shell-shocked, with a roaring pain in his middle.

In the distance, he heard sirens approaching. "Thank goodness," he breathed in relief. "Someone's coming to help." With some difficulty, he stumbled to the roadway to wait, clutching his gut in agony. The EMT truck arrived first, skidding to a stop. Two young men jumped out, grabbed their gear and raced toward the wrecked car. Alex squinched his eyes together to see better, watching in disbelief. He sat clearly in the pool of their headlights. "Hey, guys! I'm right here!" Alex yelled.

"Come back." Unhearing, the paramedics continued their urgent scramble to the silent vehicle.

"Here he is," one of them yelled. "Help me get this tree limb off the car."

"What? No! What're you doing? I'm up here on the road," Alex shouted. "Please, come help me." His breath dragged reluctantly from his lungs like a bad dog from under the bed. His plea for help still fell on deaf ears. He watched, stunned, as the two paramedics struggled to lift the heavy limb out of their way. "Come on, guys. I'm not there," he whispered painfully, his eyes filling with tears of agonizing realization. "Oh, dear God, please help me. I'm dead."

Soon, more sirens and lights brought an Allen County sheriff's deputy and a second emergency squad racing to the rescue. They too pushed past Alex, in a hurry to assist the first responders. He pleaded with each one, "Don't let me die; please don't let me die." They rushed on, ignoring him, as if he wasn't there.

Resigning himself, he watched the rescuers swarm over the vehicle. "We're gonna need the Jaws of Life," he heard one paramedic call urgently. "He's crushed into the steering wheel. I have a pulse but it's fading fast. This is not looking good. Hurry!"

It was in that precise moment that the pain left his body. He felt suddenly stronger and fitter than he had in twenty-five years. "A miracle!" he rejoiced. "It's a miracle!" He sprang to his feet to share the amazing good news with the emergency workers, stopping short as he heard the strained voice of the paramedic.

"No hurry now, guys," the man declared sadly. "He's gone. We can't help him. Call the coroner."

Alex stood silently, the exhilaration of moments ago swept away like a feather on the wind. *Is that it?* His eyes filled with tears; his lower lip quivered. *Am I really dead? I don't want to be dead.*

He watched in a stupor as the Jaws of Life sheared through the mangled steel enough for the rescuers to pull him from the wreckage. They laid his body on a gurney so the coroner could make the formal pronunciation, then loaded him into the squad for the return to Lima.

As the tow truck arrived, Alex turned away and started tramping along the snowy roadside, wondering where he was going to go now. It didn't seem to matter much. With a start, he realized that even walking in bare feet in the snow, he wasn't cold. In fact, he was quite comfortable. "Well, I suppose if I'm dead, it's at least nice to find out that it's not painful," he reasoned. "Being dead is trouble enough."

Never a religious man, Alex nevertheless found himself praying as he walked. It seemed only natural. "Dear God, nobody's going to care that I'm gone, so I really don't mind dying, I guess. But I really wanted to make it to Cambridge for Christmas Eve. It would sure be nice if you could just let me make a quick detour to poke around a little and see the light show I've heard so much about. You know, one last look around the old home place for old time's sake?"

The weirdest sensation came over him, kind of like hitting the highest point on the swings in City Park when he was a little kid. Or the time in his junior year when he had that head-on collision with the opposing linebacker during the Cambridge-Meadowbrook game, when he could've sworn his feet had lost contact with the ground. He was afraid to look. *This has been one heck of a night*, he thought. *What'll happen next?* He shook his head, which only served to heighten the strange floating feeling. He wondered if he was going to throw up again.

Almost imperceptibly at first, he sensed motion beneath his feet, as if he stood on the magic carpet of Tangu. *I haven't thought of "One Thousand and One Nights" in years—since I was a boy*, he grinned. *If I had known dying was going to be like this, I think I would've looked forward to it more.*

As his forward momentum gradually increased, Alex chanced a look down. There was no magic carpet, but…his feet *were* a few inches off the ground! *I'm flying?* He blinked, dumbfounded. *This is totally weird*, he concluded in disbelief. Gaining altitude from second to second, he freaked out a little as the earth seemed to spin away beneath him. Soon though, he realized the sensation was pleasant, surprisingly enough, almost soothing. *I could like this*, he conceded. *Don't have much choice anyway, so I guess I'll relax and enjoy the ride.*

Moonlight struck the snowy surface of the earth, illuminating the scenery below as he sped high overhead. Before long, the lights of Lima passed on his right. The streets were quiet this time of the night. Bellefontaine came into view, followed quickly by Marysville and Dublin. His speed increased by the second. *Wow, Columbus is a beautiful maze of moving white lights from up here*, he marveled.

Far below, street lights lit Interstate 70 like a giant airport runway heading east. *Now I know where I'm going*, he grinned with glee. *I'm going home!*

On through Reynoldsburg to the quiet of the countryside boroughs he flew. When he spied the Y Bridge in Zanesville, he knew he was almost home. Now dropping closer to the earth with each mile, the light pollution from Cambridge at last came into view, a whitish haze in the heavens above the town.

Almost there. Alex could barely contain his excitement. Abruptly, his flight veered north, up and over the hills, and then things really got familiar. *There's Wills Creek, and Mom and Dad's old place off Old 21 Road. Oh, that brings back such good memories.* He clearly saw every detail of the home he'd grown up in—the upstairs window screens wrapped in plastic for the winter, the broom Mom used summer and winter to sweep the porch, Dad's well-worn work boots outside the cellar entrance. *Omigosh! There they are, waving from the porch! Hi Mom, Dad! I love you!*

He tried to stop, wanting to embrace his parents again, but the force that moved him pulled him on. On, past Pleasant Valley School, the old one-room schoolhouse he'd attended as a boy. *Is that Mrs. Porter standing there with Jimmy? He was such a good brother. How I've missed him.* "Hi Jimmy! Hello, Mrs. Porter! So good to see you both again," he called as the two smiled and waved back.

Universal Potteries, where Alex worked his first job, lurched into view, stark white in the night's darkness. His solicitous old supervisor stood out on the loading dock, lighting his pipe. He waved as Alex flew by.

Veering northwest, his silent transport abruptly reentered the present on Wheeling Avenue, all lit up for the holiday season. Dickens characters huddled in chatty groups on either side of the street, inviting a return to a gentler, quieter time. The State Theatre building, where he'd entertained many a date during high school, though repurposed, still sat across from the post office, as grand as ever he remembered it. *What great memories this brings back*, thought Alex, choking back tears of happiness. *Coming home to this place is like going back in time, watching my life in review. I love this town.*

Up ahead, a throng surrounded the courthouse. Traffic weaved carefully past people in the streets. Warmly dressed citizens milled about, rubbing their hands together and tugging hoods up on their heads to keep the cold at bay. Alex was reminded of the warmth and peace he was feeling despite the cold weather and his recent demise.

He wasn't prepared for what he saw as he arrived at the square. Right on cue, the courthouse seemed to come to life. A kaleidoscope of color danced to the rhythms of Christmas carols he'd sung as a boy. He hovered transparently over the heads of the crowd, mesmerized, as children danced and people sang along beneath his feet.

Cambridge gives new meaning to the 'Christmas spirit,' he thought joyfully, unaware that his toes were keeping time to the music. *This must be the closest to heaven on earth a person could ever know. I'm so blessed to call Cambridge my hometown.*

When the lights and music stopped between shows, the mayor strode quickly up the courthouse steps. He wore a microphone on his lapel. "Ladies and gentlemen, let me have your attention for a moment, please. We had hoped a special guest would be here this evening for this most auspicious announcement, but we just got word that he won't be able to join us. I'm sure, though, that he's here in spirit."

"Some of you know Alex Butterfield, who graduated from Cambridge High School and went on in life to become a renowned chemical engineer with a body of work so substantial and influential that he's become a household name across the country. Well, recently Mr. Butterfield contacted me to say that he has funded a substantial endowment…" The crowd rose up as one body with thunderous applause. The mayor waited for it to die down. "… a substantial endowment for the ongoing improvement and maintenance of Cambridge's burgeoning downtown area. He expressed his great appreciation for all those who have pitched in to make Cambridge the revitalized, growing city it has become in recent years. He told me he wants to make sure the work continues…to the tune of twenty MILLION dollars."

It was so quiet you could hear the courthouse clock ticking. Suddenly, woolen scarves, knit caps, and little children filled the air and a rousing "HURRAH for Alex Butterfield!" rang out in the snowy square. Families turned to hug each other. The mayor wore a grin as broad as the National Road, making his way through the crowd, shaking hands and thanking folks for doing their part.

Alex felt a tear course down his cheek as he realized his time here was done. With a contented smile, he whispered a goodbye into the wind, "I guess I've done my part for my old hometown. Now I'll have to leave the rest up to you." He hoped someone was listening.

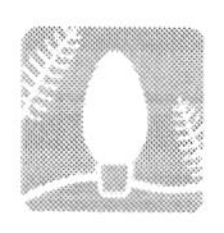

THE SIGN

"Before Tom died, we used to argue about it—heaven…the afterlife...those things," 47-year-old Meredith Snellen explained to her aisle-side seatmate, Amy. Amy was a middle-aged Delta stewardess deadheading back from London to JFK, grateful for good conversation. "We didn't really fight—just pillow talk, but we never agreed. He wasn't really an atheist or anything like that, but he always said, 'When it's over, it's over.' He didn't think there was anything more when you die. That's why he told me not to wait, to just move on. It was odd, but a week before he was killed, we talked about heaven, you know—waiting up for the other when one of us died."

Amy's eyes grew wide with expectation. Long, personal, transatlantic conversations with interesting passengers had become one of her favorite job perks. She'd never spoken with a murder victim's widow before, and the tale was growing intense!

"A week before. Oh dear, I just can't imagine," consoled Amy, pausing. "Did that help or did it make things harder?" she asked, peering at Meredith with the softest sympathy her Botoxed eyes could muster.

On a moment's reflection, Meredith replied in quiet tones, barely audible above the purr of Lockheed engines. "Both, really. I suppose that's why I fled to England—to wait. He told me I should just move on with my life when he was gone, but I told him, 'No, I think it's just like in Carousel. I'll wait.' You know, the Broadway show Carousel. *You'll Never Walk Alone*. The

Starkeeper. Holding to faith and waiting. Do you remember the story?"

"Well, some of it. It's been twenty or thirty years since I've seen it. Her husband dies young and she waits to see him in heaven. Years go by, and then she gets a sign he's still there, waiting for her, right?" Amy tried to recall the plot from scattered memories, feeling suddenly as if she were a Jeopardy contestant in search of the right question. Meredith, she noted, was still a comely blonde, pretty enough to occasionally get hit on by college kids at pubs, though perhaps when their friends weren't looking. She'd likely spent the last decade shooing away barflies.

Meredith nodded, unable to speak for a moment. She'd had to clear the lump in her throat many times over the years when talking of Tom. She sipped her drink to buy time. "Yes. That's pretty much it. We were in theater together, so we always used to make our debating points by using the shows and characters we liked. I loved to play Julie in Carousel and, once, he played Billy Bigelow. In the story, Billy dies just after their child is born. It's hard, but Julie waits for him while she raises their daughter alone. And when it really gets rough for them, years later, and they both need him, he steals a star from heaven's Starkeeper and brings it down to earth—just for a moment—to show them. Just a little sign—something to keep them going...hoping...believing." Her eyes began to moisten as she fought back tears with practiced thespian skill.

"Is that why you waited? Why you went to London?" inquired Amy, suddenly gripped with a fear that she'd asked too much. Torn between the will to know and the discretion to leave unhealed wounds alone, she drew back in hesitation.

"It's OK. I think I need to talk about this." Meredith dabbed at nose and crow's feet with a Delta napkin. Catching her breath, she continued, "Yes. The problem was, he always fought back with another musical: Hello, Dolly! Do you remember that one? Just like Julie in Carousel, I always loved to play Dolly too. And Tom played Horace Vandergelder. Do you remember?"

"Just the show tunes, some of them, I think. Streisand did the movie, right?" Amy prayed her second Jeopardy question answer showed adequate theatrical intelligence.

"Yes. Walter Matthau played Horace. Dolly is this really vibrant, childless matchmaker who fixes everyone up but herself. It's like she can't move on without Ephraim, her husband—like she's waiting for him and doesn't know what to do."

Meredith hesitated, then spoke in a forlorn whisper, "But then she does move on with this guy who really needs her, Horace Vandergelder. There's a song—*Before the Parade Passes By*. Oh, I *loved* it when Tom played Horace to my Dolly! It never felt right with any other man. It felt so much like...well, like back when we got engaged in college. It felt like our wedding day too." A second napkin damped away tears.

"So Dolly moved on, but Julie didn't." Amy thought a moment as Meredith fought to regain her composure. "I think I see the problem." With Jeopardy-worthy Shakespearean insight, Amy built an analogy. "It's like Hamlet: 'To be, or not to be,' except for you, it's 'To move on, or not to move on.' That *is* the question, isn't it?" Amy leaned closer, anticipating the 'Yes.'

"Yes. I think that's most of why I moved to London. I didn't know it for a while. At first, I was so angry I couldn't see straight. I just didn't want to be anywhere near it—the wreckage on the ground, or the hole when they cleared it. They never found him, you know. Not even a little baked bone. Not a wisp of anything they could put into a test tube and tell me it was a man worth burying. He just vanished into the air. The air is in London, you know, just the same as in New York. I only think of him when I breathe." An eruptive, heartbroken laugh sprang from

Meredith's lips, the fruit of a bittersweet joke with too much truth behind it.

"It took a couple of years to think about anything else, it seemed. I just kept breathing...breathing...breathing... Sure, I was working too—hitting the mark, projecting my lines, wandering back to a cheap flat in Covent Garden. I just kept on breathing. I breathed at night too. You know how I know that?" Her face crinkled toward a what-else-can-I-do expression.

"You dreamed about him, didn't you?" Amy spoke with sureness and a comforting serenity in her voice. This was a different sort of Jeopardy question, the kind any woman could answer.

"Yes. Dreams...nightmares...but some very good dreams at times. Those were the ones that kept me in bed half the day, trying to keep sleep going. Have you ever been in a dream and tried to stay there—wakened up just enough to know that the world isn't where you're meant to be, so you pull the dream back like a life preserver? You squeeze your eyes shut and hang on for dear life to sleep."

"Yes, it's happened to me too, but nothing like what you've gone through." Amy was on firm ground now. All women know days when dreams seem better than light.

"Anyhow, it took a few years to get over the anger. After that, I suppose I was just hiding."

"Is there a 'Horace Vandergelder' in your life now? Is that why you're going back, like Dolly?" Amy asked, firmly grasping the thread of theatrical metaphors.

"No. It's just time. I think I've been hiding from 'Horace,' if there's one in the world for me. Not that I don't think well of British actors, but I've just felt safer from 'Horace' around men with bad teeth." They both guffawed at the stereotype.

"You're safe telling that part to an American!" Amy smirked with a guilty grin. As the laughter died and thoughts returned to the story, Amy shot a probing question. "So in the play, what made Dolly move on?"

"Funny you should ask that. Tom didn't believe in an afterlife, really. He always said I'd have to move on like Dolly—before the parade passed me by. But that's where I got him back. You see, Dolly waits for a sign from her husband up in heaven, showing that he's blessed her to take a new husband. *'What about that!'* I'd say to Tom, triumphantly. 'It's *still* like Carousel. You have to wait for a sign!' Then we'd laugh like a couple of loony birds because we knew—we just *knew*—we were never going to die." Meredith stared disparagingly at the crumpled wad of tissue in her hand. "May I borrow your napkin, Amy?"

"I was 37, and he was 39. We'd had a wonderful twenty years together, ever since the day I met him playing Don Quixote at a little place called the Barn Theater, just outside Cambridge, my hometown in Ohio. I was a senior in high school and he was a gallant sophomore at Muskingum College, just a few miles away. We loved playing summer stock together. The Saturday after *my* Muskingum graduation, we got married. Say, do you know Man of La Mancha?"

"Absolutely!' Amy grinned, leaping at the question. "It's one of my favorites. I just watched a BBC production on layover last month!" Affecting the stance of a tiger poised to strike, she quizzed, "And I'll bet you played Dulcinea!"

"How did you ever guess?!" They laughed, as it seemed a deep bond was forming. "Yes, I was Tom's Dulcinea. He loved being Don Quixote. No one ever sang *The Impossible Dream* better! The odd thing is...he dies in that one too. Carousel; Hello, Dolly!; Man of La Mancha. The plays we loved were all about widows. I saw the pattern later, but I should have seen it coming! I was in L.A. that week, doing a commercial. On Monday, Tom's agent called the apartment to say he had a shot at Masterpiece Theater...as Don Quixote—the star! He asked Tom to meet him at the top floor restaurant in the north tower the next morning." She paused. "Only thing was...that was the morning the planes came too."

Sound science says you can't hear a pin drop on a noisy jet plane, yet Amy felt the silence of pins wash over her. A long pause ensued, broken by a question. "Was that the end? Did you ever learn anything more?"

"Only what the answering machine told me. I didn't even know he'd gone there—just that he didn't answer the phone that day, nor on any day ever, ever again," explained Meredith. "We were saving up to have a baby on just Tom's income, so we only had the one cell phone. His message said it was hot and there was a lot of smoke, and he was going to try to make it to the roof. His last words—and he was breathing heavy and fast, you know—were 'I love you. I've got to go now.' That's all I know. He's in the air. That's all I know," she shrugged. "He didn't tell me who to be—Julie...or Dolly...or even Dulcinea. What good's a leading lady without her script?"

Amy nodded, her own breaths growing deeper.

"I still don't understand it, but a strange little letter I got last month seemed like a nudge toward moving on. I'd been holding out for a sign—something big, something that blazed across the sky like a comet or a big, fat dinosaur-killing meteor!" Meredith sighed. "You know, Amy, I don't really know where this plane of yours is taking me. All my belongings are packed up and headed for a Staten Island storage bin. I think I'm going to go back to the old neighborhood in Brooklyn for a while. I'll pick up some off-Broadway work, or even do sets if I have to. But first I've got to stop back in Ohio."

"Your hometown?" Amy guessed, no longer keeping score.

"That's right. I got that little letter inviting me back—some sort of presentation to high school kids about working abroad. Apparently someone thinks my London gig is exotic. Houdini's wife only waited ten years, you know, waited to see a sign. Then she gave up. Statute of limitations, I suppose. At least I waited a few months longer. Anyhow, the letter was telling me, 'Come home now.' So I'm going."

An hour later, a fine traveling friendship, cemented at 30,000 feet by epoxied revelation, came to its customary tarmac-level, day-or-a-lifetime pause point that Amy knew so well. Each exchanged an e-mail address with the other, both knowing that the odds were against their use. Meredith, the fugitive actress, and Amy, the soul-peering stewardess, parted ways with a mutual wave.

The challenge of return met Meredith sooner than expected, the very next day, as she read the Daily Jeffersonian's notice that an ingathering of Barn Theater alumni had been called for the day before Christmas: "Reception at the Cambridge Performing Arts Center, 7 p.m.; caroling at 8." The thought of seeing so many old friends, and going for the first time ever without Tom, was paralyzing. Things felt so incomplete. The emptiness returned as she drifted onto the courthouse square at half past six. A bench there beckoned, such a wonderful place to build up one's nerve. Memories of one Don Quixote played like faded snapshots, *The Impossible Dream* sounding in her mind.

'To bear with unbearable sorrow.' Yes, she knew what that line meant. 'To run where the brave dare not go.' Perhaps, she thought, in his final moments. 'To right the unrightable wrong.' She couldn't see how. 'To love pure and chaste from afar.' She'd tried so hard. 'To reach the unreachable star.' It all led back to Carousel, to Dolly, and to poor Dulcinea. She lost track of time.

As luck, fate, or Providence would have it, a pleasant man peculiarly addicted to staring at the heavens sat on a bench nearby. Noticing both the time on his watch and Meredith's so-solemn reverie, he raised an arm to point out the sky spot where he knew a glinting satellite would come by shortly. And those who watched for it saw the flash—most brilliant—which all the others missed. Moments later, Meredith rose, paused, and then stepped lively toward reunion with friends, faith, and a life that was meant to be lived.

A Hometown Prayer

John Woodley heaved the suitcase upon the bed and looked about him. "My home for the next five days," he muttered to himself. A card on the nightstand greeted him with: "Welcome to Cambridge, Ohio. Enjoy your stay at Serenity Inn." John opened the drapes to allow the late afternoon sun to brighten the modest room. *Back in the old hometown,* he thought, surveying congested Southgate Parkway. *Cambridge always was the small town with the big-city traffic.*

John recalled his childhood in the south side of Cambridge. His father was a factory worker and his mother worked part-time at Kresge's lunch counter. Money was tight, but his family was more fortunate than many others. When John was ten, his best friend's father shot himself to death when the factory that employed him closed. On that day, John swore that he would never depend upon anyone else for his livelihood. He also vowed that someday he would be wealthy and rescue his parents from the daily drudgery of manual labor. Little did he know to what extent he would keep those promises.

At the age of fifty-three, John was one of Hollywood's most successful directors. Two Oscars sat upon his mantel and countless other awards decorated his 28-room Brentwood estate. He was the father of eleven-year-old twin sons and was married to a beautiful former actress fifteen years his junior. His first megahit, *The Crimson Endeavor,* made him a multi-millionaire at the age of twenty-four. Soon afterward, he moved his parents to a condo in Tampa, complete with servants, and wisely invested his money. Lavish spending and the Hollywood party scene were not in his plans. The kid from the Southside had made the big time.

John entered the tiny bathroom, a mere five feet from the double bed, splashed water onto his face, then stared into the mirror. The beard he had decided to grow in September was now the desired length and fullness, but the copious amount of gray surprised him. *How did I not notice it before?* he wondered.

Gray hairs were not the only bane John had been facing of late. Although he still claimed moderate success with his movies, he had not made a blockbuster for over four years. Tabloid headlines like "John Woodley—MIA at Oscars Again," bothered him more than he could admit to himself.

Although his marriage to Darlene was remarkably stable by Hollywood standards, John missed the spontaneity and energy that dominated their early years together. John knew that he had a family and life that other men could only dream of, but still he felt that something was missing. Then he would feel guilty for feeling that way. Talk-therapy and medications did not help; in fact, they only amplified the feeling that he was undeserving of his success.

When John received the invitation to speak at the symposium in Cambridge, he nearly choked on the olive in his martini. *Of course! When in doubt, go back to your roots!* To find his future path, John would return to his past and the forces that had molded him so long ago in the picturesque community that seemed a universe away.

Darlene already had planned to take the boys to Aspen just before Christmas. John told her he wished to stay in Cambridge alone for a few days and would join them in Aspen afterward. He then mapped out his plan.

John would not enter Guernsey County in a motorcade worthy of a president. No, he would return to his hometown as humbly as he had left it. When he wished to travel anonymously, he did so as "Don Cabot," an alias he borrowed from a very minor character in one of his movies. Mr. Cabot dressed in off-the-rack clothing (usually jeans), wore running shoes everywhere, sported bifocals on his face, and was bearded. This persona had fooled the paparazzi for years and John intended to use the guise to rediscover Cambridge. His rental car was a Ford Focus and his motel was inconspicuous as a mouse in a cornfield. No one would suspect that a world-renowned celebrity was gadding about the hills of southeastern Ohio.

John finger-combed the mop of curls on his head and buttoned his parka. *A couple of Coney dogs and a donut from Kennedy's will send me back like a time machine*, he thought as he strutted down the hall to the parking lot.

An hour later John emerged from Theo's Restaurant still "m-m-m-ing" audibly. *I'd forgotten how good Coney dogs are,* he thought, wondering if they could be shipped to California. A man at the counter had engaged John ("Don") in a conversation about changes Cambridge had undergone. "The Kresge building burned down a few years back," John heard as his heart sank. The man also spoke of "Victorian people" and a "courthouse light show," but John was only half-listening then. *Kresge's gone?* Some of the happiest times of his childhood were in that toy-loaded store. And his mom always sneaked him a free Coke at the lunch counter. As he ambled up Wheeling Avenue, he wondered what else Cambridge had lost.

John was deep in thought when he nearly bumped into someone. "Oh, excuse me, ma'am," he apologized before realizing he was speaking to a mannequin. He laughed upon determining that the "woman" in fancy attire was one of the Victorian people the man in the restaurant had mentioned. John gazed about the familiar downtown and was impressed with the scenes. *Some of my best set managers would be amazed*, he thought. Horse-drawn carriages decked with festive lights clip-clopped down the streets John had once pedaled on his bicycle.

That man in Theo's said something about a light show at the courthouse. I'll mosey up that way and check it out.

Nearly everyone he passed greeted him with a warm smile or a friendly "hi." A man in Victorian garb, complete with a top hat, bellowed a hearty, "'Tis a wonderful evening, sir!" and handed John a bookmark with the words to "Silent Night" printed on it. John laughed aloud at the holiday wonderland around him. "My Cambridge," he muttered. "If only Mom and Dad could see it now. Whose idea was this?"

As he crossed West Eighth Street and approached the courthouse, John observed a crowd gathering for the light show. John had seen similar shows in Russia and Germany on a much grander scale. However, the thrill of seeing his hometown's courthouse bathed in flashing, pulsating lights made this a sight worth waiting for.

He glanced at his watch. Eight-twenty. Another forty minutes before the show. He looked at the stately building he had not seen in decades. It was exactly how he remembered it. The stone steps towered like a pyramid toward the massive front doors.

In high school, John had enrolled in a photography class taught by a retired newspaper editor. For an assignment John was vaguely instructed to photograph "emotions." John assumed that anyone leaving a courthouse would be exuding emotions, so with his camera in hand he perched on the same stone steps he was seeing now. His first subject was a bee-hived woman carrying newly signed divorce papers. When she saw John aiming his camera at her, she jumped into the air with arms raised and shouted, "I'm a free woman!" *That was emotion*, John remembered with a smile.

Another time, he was standing with his camera at the side door of the courthouse, waiting for a prisoner to be escorted back to jail. The man had been convicted of a brutal crime and was not at all happy with the verdict. He attempted to attack the judge, prompting the deputies to subdue and carry him to the jailhouse down the alley. When the convict saw John with his camera, he stopped screaming long enough to shout, "I'll come back for you, kid! You're dead meat!" John never told the story to anyone, but he had nightmares for weeks afterward.

With time to kill, John decided to explore the immediate vicinity. The old cannon was still there. New monuments covered the area just east of the Soldiers and Sailors statue. *So many wars*, he thought as the gray feeling of emptiness began creeping into his mind again.

John distracted himself by concentrating on an A-framed object positioned at the sidewalk's edge. He walked to the front to see what was displayed in the oddly-shaped contraption.

"A nativity scene!" John said aloud, mildly shocked. *I haven't seen one of these in years. I know Cambridge is backward, but everyone knows this is not politically correct!*

After overcoming his initial reaction to the "outdated" display, John's critical director's eye took command. *They could at least make an attempt to be accurate*, he mused. *Mary and Joseph are white as snow and have English features.* John leaned for a closer look at Baby Jesus. *Oh, yeah, you really want your God to have chipped plaster on his ear and painted hair that makes him look like a carnival game prize. And again—what's with the porcelain white skin? He was Middle-Eastern: make him brown, or at least tan. Do you think he came from Sweden?*

John stifled a laugh as he reveled in his role as critic, but was jolted from the reverie when a voice directly behind him said, "He is everywhere and everything." John spun around to see who had been watching him. No one else was in the area. The nearest person was a young woman selling hot chocolate about fifteen feet away. John scanned the faces in the crowd but no one was looking at him.

He attempted to dispel the feeling of uneasiness by concentrating on the Baby Jesus. *He doesn't look so white now,* he thought. *In fact, the plaster looks exactly like human skin!*

Suddenly, the little figure with outstretched arms began to glow, taking the appearance of a baby-shaped nightlight. John observed the footlights that illuminated the display, but quickly realized that the source was within the baby. The glow became brighter, mesmerizing John so that all other stimuli were blocked from his consciousness. Then, before his very eyes, the Christ figure transformed into a living, squirming, blond child with rosy cheeks. The next second, the child's skin became dark brown, his head covered with black curls. Almost instantly, the child's hair then became straight and black, and his facial features were Oriental. A mere second later, the child lying in the straw-filled manger took on the unmistakable characteristics of a person from the Middle East. Within a few seconds, the child was once again only a plaster figure in a man-made Christmas display.

John trembled. He knew he did not imagine the transformations. He also knew that the voice he had heard was real. Chills ran up his spine as he gathered his thoughts. *I was chosen to witness a miracle. But why? Why me?*

John felt a warmness envelop him, almost like the hugs his mother gave him when he first started school. With sudden clarity, he realized what had been missing in his life. As he lowered himself to his knees, the feelings of depression and anxiety that had been haunting him vanished. "Thank you, Lord," he whispered while bowing his head.

Then John did something he had not done since his youthful days in Cambridge. He prayed.

THE HARD WAY HOME

JERRY WOLFROM

Joe Powers put down the tequila bottle and squinted into the gathering darkness. The big cat was crouched behind the sandstone boulders, eying the water tanks in the ravine. Joe had found two dead calves, gutted and half-eaten. As an "enforcer" for three large ranches, his job was to track down and kill coyotes and cougars that preyed on the cattle and sheep.

His mule, Luke, twitched nervously at the clattering from the rusty windmill that pumped water into the tanks. In addition to wild animals, the water also attracted illegals, or "wets" as they were called in border areas, who had slipped across the Arizona-Mexican border ten miles south. It was also Joe's job to scare off the "wets" with a few bursts from his AK-47. He never aimed to hit any of them, just turn them around and send them frantically scrambling across the parched desert to search for another path north.

It was a lonely life in the remote desert, but that's how Joe chose to live. He usually stayed a week camping in the harsh area in search of four-legged marauders. After that, he would return to his dilapidated one-room camper parked behind Pancho's Bar in tiny Cactus Hill. Generally, he traveled the unforgiving terrain in his 1989 pickup truck, sleeping in the bed with his four tri-colored Walker tracking hounds. This time, because the desert floor was so rocky, he walked with Luke, his pack mule. The dogs were resting back at his camper.

In the dim light of dusk, Joe saw a dark shadow, then the vague outline of the cat warily approaching the water tanks. His

Weatherby belched twice, spinning the cat around. It wasn't a kill, but Joe knew one of his heavy .300 caliber slugs had found its mark. The cat would drag itself off and be dead by morning.

Bone-tired, the grisly hunter unrolled his sleeping bag and wiggled inside. He removed a crumpled paper from his tattered jeans and, by lantern light, reread the letter inviting him to the Cambridge symposium during the Christmas break. Scribbled across the bottom was, "We know you can't discuss your military career, but your input into the tribulations of overseas travel would be invaluable."

Ridiculous! Travel twenty-five hundred miles to a snowbound hometown for a Christmas symposium? *Not a chance.* At daybreak, Joe had Luke begin the trek back to Cactus Hill. Seven miles of treacherous, rocky footing. *Cambridge at Christmastime*, he mused. He hadn't been home in years, despite the fact that his estranged wife, Eve, lived there and he owned two parcels of valuable land in Jackson Township, left to him by his parents.

While he could sell the land and have enough money on which to retire, Joe had less than four hundred dollars hidden in the wall of his camper. He doubted that the money would get him to Cambridge, and the chance of his rusty truck lasting all the way without blowing up were slim to none. *Still...*

Christmas had not been an important part of Joe's life since his parents died and he left Cambridge. The only family he knew was his army buddies, with whom he had spent countless Christmas Eves in hostile, dangerous parts of the world. But somehow the symposium letter and its mention of the holidays sparked some latent memories. He smiled as his mind rewound back to his high school days. He had been a good student, but mischievous. Joe was always among the usual suspects.

After graduation, he enrolled in Green Mountain College, a little-known school in Vermont, where he majored in adventure education. That curriculum focused on wildlife management, the environment, and outdoor survival. Joe relished two-week camping trips to remote Vermont mountains in the dead of harsh winters. He also enjoyed the time when his class struggled for survival in the jungles along the Amazon River. It seemed natural after graduation that he join the Army and try for a Special Forces unit.

Eventually, he was assigned to Blue Nine and sent to Bosnia. Over the next years, his covert twelve-man unit served in Mogadishu, Kazakhstan, Uzbekistan, Iraq, and Pakistan. Between two of those assignments while on leave in the United States, he married Eve, a lovely woman who was a surgical nurse. *Darling Eve, the perfect wife*. But Eve couldn't cope with his long overseas absences and the hard-bitten attitude that came with his work. Neither of them suggested a divorce; they would just remain friends. *Maybe someday...*

Joe plodded across the mesa, leading Luke. Just a mile now from Cactus Hill. His legs felt like lead. He fought back hallucinations and fatigue in the scorching sun. He gargled down the last inch of tequila in the bottle, then tossed it into the brush. Even Luke was exhausted and limping. *Too old for this life*, Joe admitted to himself. Now past his fifty-fifth birthday, the solitary tracker lifestyle had taken its toll. For the first time, he pondered dying alone, somewhere in the rugged desert or mountains of Cochise County.

The usual patrons at Pedro's, mostly Mexicans, gave Joe a noisy welcome. "Man, you don't look like that picture on the wall," Sanchez quipped. "You're a mess, amigo."

Joe's bloodshot eyes glanced at the pencil drawing of him a professional artist had made a few years back. He wore a John Wayne cavalry hat and had a crooked smile on his craggy face. Everyone who saw it noticed his resemblance to Clark Gable in Gable's last picture, "The Misfits." Joe smiled. No resemblance now. He hadn't shaved in three weeks; his mostly-gray, stringy hair hung down to his shoulders. Willy Nelson, perhaps.

"Want your usual double tequila?" Pedro asked, reaching for a bottle on the bottom shelf.

"No," Joe shot back. "I'm quitting. No more booze. I'm on the wagon."

"What brought that on?" the astonished Pedro asked.

"That stuff is killing me. I'm done with it. Besides, I'm taking off in the morning for Ohio. Home for Christmas." He couldn't believe he said it. "No more sleeping on hard rocks and freezing up in the high country. I spent the last three Christmas Eves eating cold beans, chewing on a chunk of jerky, and finishing it off with a candy bar and a pint of worm juice."

"Nobody goes to Ohio in the winter," one of the Hispanics offered. "They got a big storm up there right now. You gonna fly?"

"I'm driving," Joe said, heading unsteadily for the door. "Gomez, take care of my dogs and Luke. And tell your wife she can have my camper for a chicken coop."

Turning onto Interstate 10 at Willcox, Joe would stay in the South as long as possible because of the weather. The old truck was running hot. Just inside the New Mexico line, the engine made a couple of sickening coughs, followed by the unmistakable smell of burned oil, accompanied by a radiator geyser. The old relic could go no further. Joe pushed it into the ditch and stuck out his thumb.

In a matter of minutes, an old rancher stopped to give him a ride west. A half-hour later, Joe got out to walk to a tiny airstrip with Chaparral Air painted on a small hanger.

"I'm leaving for Houston," the manager said. "I already got one passenger, but I can make room for you. A hundred bucks."

"Where's the other passenger?"

"Already loaded. A dead oil field guy in a casket."

Joe peeled the bills from off his meager four hundred dollar stash, then slipped into the little plane. The pilot said little during the first hour, but somewhere over west Texas, he turned to Joe and calmly said, "I can't hold her up. We're going down."

Fortunately, they had been flying at a low altitude. The plane dropped slowly, eventually leveling off as the pilot skillfully maneuvered it to a crash landing that tore off the landing gears. After belly-sliding for a few hundred feet in the soft, red sand, the plane stopped. The pilot, Joe, and the man in the casket were unscathed.

It was much like two helicopter "hard landings" that Joe had survived in Iraq. "End of the line," the pilot muttered. "You can probably catch a bus in Fort Stockton, it's just over that rim."

"How about a rebate?" Joe asked. "I paid you to get me to Houston."

"Not a chance," the pilot said defensively, shaking his head. "I got to buy new landing gears."

Joe walked the two miles to Fort Stockton and bought a bus ticket to St. Louis; his bankroll was dwindling. More worrisome was that Christmas was just three days away.

Tossing his old duffle bag into the Greyhound's baggage compartment, he settled in for the long ride to St. Louis. Hopefully, he could sleep much of the way—and hopefully his remaining money would be enough to buy a bus ticket to Cambridge. It was a gamble, but Joe's entire adult life had been a gamble in one way or another.

The bus made a short rest stop at a small town deep in the Ozarks. Finding a telephone booth, Joe called a surprised Eve, who could barely speak. Still, she was excited at his return to Cambridge. "Of course, you will stay with me," she said, with contagious enthusiasm. Joe felt a warm glow at the sound of her voice. "You should talk to a developer here who's interested in buying your land."

"Fine. I guess those two parcels are worth almost a hundred thousand."

"Try two hundred and fifty thousand," Eve giggled.

Stunned, Joe finally managed to reply. "All the more reason to get there in a hurry. I'll call you soon." Now he couldn't wait to get home.

A depressing rain was pelting down and a light fog settling in when the bus resumed its journey toward St. Louis. But 20 minutes later the driver shouted, "Watch it!" Then came the horrifying grinding crash as an oncoming semi rig, drifting left of center, sideswiped the bus. After the sickening crash of metal against metal, the disabled Greyhound nosed down a shallow hill, coming to rest in a grove of small pine trees. Everyone was badly shaken up, but there were no injuries.

After a frenzied cell phone call, the near-hysterical driver announced that a replacement bus was on its way.

In St. Louis, Joe found he was twenty-four dollars short of bus fare to Cambridge. He walked down the rain-swept street, not quite able to break the habit of checking rooftops for snipers. Two blocks away, he found a truck stop with about twenty big rigs lined up in the parking lot. An old Peterbilt with a lighted American flag on the grill caught his eye. On the trailer were stickers indicating the independent driver was a former Marine, a Vietnam veteran, and a member of the American Legion.

The driver left the café, headed for the truck. "Semper Fi," Joe greeted him. Ralph, according to the patch on his jacket, returned the salute. Joe removed from his wallet his Army papers and handed them to Ralph.

"Great," Ralph said. "What outfit?"

"Army. Special Ops, mostly in the Middle East. You headed east?"

Ralph nodded. "Going to Pittsburgh with a light load of appliance parts. Where you going?"

"Cambridge, Ohio, if you'll give me a lift."

Shaking his head at Joe's filthy jeans, battered cowboy hat, scuffed boots, scraggly hair, and unkempt beard, Ralph shrugged. "I go right through Cambridge on this run. Climb up. Looks like you're on your last legs. You can crash in the sleeper. It's kind of a boar's nest, but the mattress is soft."

Eight hours later, Joe awoke with a start. "I must have died," he moaned groggily.

"You slept through two pit stops," Ralph laughed. Handing Joe two large cheeseburgers and a Coke, he added, "We just cleared Zanesville, so you're practically home, partner."

Joe was on his second cheeseburger when Ralph swore loudly, "I think we're on fire. Smell it?" More swearing.

Joe replied, "Yup. Burning rubber and diesel fuel."

Ralph hit the brakes, then quickly steered the rig to the berm just as flames shot upward from the big engine. "Get out of here," he ordered. "This thing's one hot mamma."

Within minutes, an ambulance, two fire trucks, and three state patrol cars arrived. The cab was fully engulfed in angry fire and black smoke. Later, while a crowd of onlookers watched the wrecker haul the Peterbilt away, one patrolman said to another, "Things are under control here. I'm headed back to Cambridge to check out."

Joe grinned feebly. "I don't look so good, but I need a lift to Cambridge. I've had a heckova time trying to get from Arizona to be home for Christmas. I'm twenty years late."

The patrolman glanced at Ralph, who gave nodding approval. "Let's go," he said, adding later, "You're not going to recognize Cambridge."

"No?"

"They've turned the town into a holiday showcase," the cop said. "Dickens statues on Wheeling Avenue, tour buses from all over, all kind of activities, and a spectacular lighted courthouse."

"A lighted courthouse?"

"You have to see all the stuff to believe it," the officer smiled.

Eve was backing out of her driveway when the state patrol car pulled up. Her first look was one of horror, then fear until she finally recognized Joe. No longer a spit-and-polish soldier, he looked one of the transients who made their home under the viaduct.

"Do you know this man?" the cop asked in a professional tone.

Eve raced to embrace Joe gingerly. "I'm pretty sure that after he has a bath, a haircut, and a shave and I get him into some decent clothes that he may be a husband I haven't seen in years," she cried out, almost in tears.

The officer smiled. "Merry Christmas," he said, easing his cruiser from the curb.

A Feeling Long Forgotten

"Hold your arm out, Mama, I wanta take your pulse," instructed the little pigtailed girl.

"Oh, okay. Are you a nurse?"

"No, Mama. I'm a doctor. When I grow up, I'm gonna make sick people all better."

Such lofty ambitions, thought her mother. *With my son, I don't see much chance of anything even close to that ever happening, but with this one, who knows? I have never seen a child with such determination once she gets something in her head. There's no dissuading her; she'll just dig in her heels and work for anything she wants.*

"Okay, Sweetie, if that's what you want, chances are, that's what you'll do."

And that's just what Jennifer White did.

She was the youngest child of widowed Marie White, an industrious woman who owned a small but successful home and office cleaning business.

No job was too large or too small for White's Squeaky-Clean services. The hours were long and tiring but, as each of Marie's children became old enough, they assisted their mother in the family enterprise while they attended school.

As Jennifer approached graduation, she became more certain she wanted to attend medical school. She often sought the advice of the family doctor, who recommended she do some volunteer work at Guernsey Memorial Hospital. That did it! As a candy striper she felt that she was in her element.

Jennifer exclaimed to her mother, "Mom, I want to be a doctor so much. I know it's very expensive and takes a very long time. My grades have been good; I think I might be able to get some small scholarships but, even with your help and me working, it won't be enough."

Marie answered thoughtfully. "Honey, I've been giving this a lot of thought. I'm going to make a suggestion, something for you to consider. Have you thought about joining one of the armed services? You'd get a good start on your education, get some experience, maybe even travel a bit, and serve your country, all at the same time. After a four year stint it wouldn't take long to get your bachelors,' then you could enter medical school."

Jennifer looked at her mother in amazement. "No," she replied. "It never entered my mind. But it makes sense. I believe I'll talk to some recruiters. It couldn't hurt."

During the next few days, Jennifer "made the rounds," collecting brochures and verbal information on the U.S. Army, Air Force, and Navy. She and her mother studied the data over the next few weeks, weighing the opportunities being offered by the various services. Jennifer, once again, visited each of the recruiters. Finally, she made a decision. She would join the Air Force upon graduating high school.

In July of that year, the summer of 1980, Jennifer Marie White reported for duty at Lackland Air Force Base for basic training. She was scared, but excited to be starting on the road to becoming a medical doctor and the new experiences ahead of her.

And what an experience basic was. Texas was hot and dusty, the training rigorous and difficult. *What was I thinking? Joining up this time of year when I knew I'd be coming to Texas? I must have been out of my mind!*

And then homesickness reared its ugly head. Jennifer could hardly wait to get out of basic so she could visit relatives in San Antonio. Her mother's sister and her family all lived around the area. It would be great to spend some time with them, see the sights, and catch up on the family. But for now she would have to bear the oppressive heat and exhausting basic training. After all, it was the first step to becoming a doctor.

After finishing her stint in the Air Force, Jennifer entered Ohio State University, where she received her B.S., then on to Case Western University, where she finally received her heart's desire. She was now Jennifer Marie White, M.D., General Practitioner.

Jennifer had given a lot of thought to her future during those few years. Getting her degree was one thing, how to use it was another. She went home to Cambridge and once again consulted her mother.

"I know, this sounds crazy, Mama, but I've been thinking about maybe rejoining the Air Force. Once I was out of basic, I loved the experiences, the traveling, and the people I met. I'm sure I could get a commission and, from information I've received, they need doctors."

"Well," said Marie, "I guess you've given this considerable thought and explored the pros and cons. I can see where it could work out very well for you. Do you plan to make it a career or just do a stint?"

A career in the Air Force looked very appealing to Jennifer; she planned to use her medical knowledge to the best of her ability.

"I'm very proud of you, Honey. I'm sure you're making the right decision for you," said Marie. "You know I'll support you in any way I can."

And so it was that Major Jennifer Marie White found herself in Afghanistan when the letter arrived. She had had the honor of serving in the Air Force for more than fifteen years in several countries and as many different bases.

Along the way, she had the opportunity to take classes at some of the finest medical schools in the Europe; Vrige Universiteit in Brussels; Charles University, Prague; St. George University of London; University of Limoges, France; University of Eastern Piedmont, Italy; and many others.

She became fluent in several languages and developed friends wherever she went. To say that Jennifer White found a "home in the Air Force" would be putting it mildly. She seldom thought of Cambridge, or even Ohio. Her mother had died ten years earlier and her brother had taken over the family business. They corresponded through emails and occasional phone calls but that was her only connection there.

And now here she was, half a world away, reading an invitation to attend a symposium on global travel to be held in Cambridge in December. She guessed she would certainly qualify to address the subject. *Well, I have furlough time coming but I have no desire to go to Cambridge on my time off. No, I'm planning to visit Spain and doing a little sightseeing with friends before reporting for my next duty station. It'll be great to get out of here.*

With that thought, Jennifer tossed the invitation into a wastebasket and went to bed.

The next morning found her very tired and somewhat disturbed. Having not slept well, she couldn't pinpoint the reason for her uneasiness.

Bad dreams. No, I don't think so. But what's wrong with me? Touching her forehead, she felt no sign of fever. Pulse normal. Preparing a light breakfast of coffee and toast, she yawned as she tried to shake the weird feelings.

As she slowly awakened, a strange feeling came over her and she began thinking of her parents and her brother. *How odd that my childhood should come to mind.* At the same time, a warm feeling enveloped her, like she was wrapped in love and kindness and…*something else...what is that?* It was a feeling she hadn't experienced for a long time and she couldn't identify it.

I've got to pull myself together and get to work. I have many flyboys to see today. There's a lot of cold and flu going around. Maybe that's my problem, but I don't seem to have the symptoms. In a couple weeks, I'll be leaving for Spain and I need to get moving.

As Jennifer made rounds, she found herself thinking more and more of her family. It had been a happy childhood, though her father died when she was just fourteen. A good man and sadly missed, his death followed a long and debilitating illness.

Thinking back to her younger years, many people came to mind, many not thought of in ages. This brought on thoughts of "wonder whatever became of…" A wave of nostalgia swept over her as she remembered friends from school and the many good times they enjoyed together. These thoughts reminded her of grade school and high school, ball diamonds, football fields, Cambridge City Park and Friday night dances. And those great family restaurants…good food at reasonable prices. There seemed to be a church or a gas station on about every corner and, scattered around the town, at that time, were still a few little neighborhood grocery stores.

And now, that elusive feeling came over her again. The one she couldn't identify. Continuing her thoughts on her growing-up years, she remembered the neighborhood kids playing in each others' back yards and how all the moms sort of looked after everyone's kids. *That's it! Safe. That's the feeling I always had. It was family, the people, the familiar buildings, the streets, and those old Guernsey County hills that wrapped themselves round me and kept me safe. No matter what was going on in the world, I always felt safe...protected.*

As Jennifer's thoughts returned more and more to home, she knew why she hadn't been able to identify the feeling. She hadn't felt this way for years. She had been so busy running to other places and looking for new experiences, she had lost something vital to her very being.

I must have left little Jennifer back there. I need to go back and visit her, that place, and those people who made me...well...me. Then maybe I can have that feeling, that safe feeling, again.

Digging the invitation out of the wastebasket, Jennifer softly giggled to herself as her thoughts jumped ahead to Christmas in Cambridge. She wondered if Santa would appear at the J.C. Penney store.

A Christmas Kiss

Early morning was Riley's favorite time of day. The cool fall breezes, mixed with the salty, pungent smell of the ocean, revived his soul and mind as he strolled the beach. Ocracoke Island, normally a bustling place with tourists, was practically deserted this time of the year. Only the permanent residents remained. Now was their time to rest, enjoy the Christmas holidays, and prepare for next season.

Reaching the end of his walk, Riley paused to scan the beach. The sun was rising over the ocean. Along the beach, small wisps of smoke rose from last night's campfires. Most of the island's business was conducted around these campfires. More planning was done in these impromptu meetings than in any Chamber of Commerce meeting. One by one, lights flickered on in the houses bordering the beach. The island was beginning to awaken.

Everyone knew everyone here. Folks simply knew him as Riley Ashton, a divorced international investment banker who made a fortune in Apple computers, then retired to the islands at age fifty. Little did they know Riley was a bestselling author, writing under the pen name of Donald Wyatt. His detective series, Max Brant, P.I., had been on the New York Times best seller list for sixteen weeks.

Startled from his mesmerizing thoughts by a low flying seagull, Riley headed back to his beachfront home. He still had to finish his latest novel.

Turning on his computer, he spotted the familiar logo of his sister, Shelby. *Better see what's going on in Cambridge, Ohio*, he thought, clicking on the icon. Shelby's letters were practically all the same, going on about the kids, her husband's used car business, and a lot of gossip. Toward the end, her letter took an all too familiar twist. *"Riley, why don't you come home for Christmas? It would be good to see you and there is a symposium at the high school for former grads that have worked and traveled the world. I think you would enjoy it."*

Riley hadn't been to Cambridge for twenty years. Pausing, he thought, *Why not? I can fly there in a few hours. Actually, I'll need a break after I finish this book.*

Two weeks later, after sending his novel to his publisher, Riley made plans to fly to Ohio. A few days before Christmas, he packed a small bag, called the local airport, and asked them to roll out the old 180 Cessna. Built in the early fifties, she was the last of the tail dragger models. He had purchased her from a pilot who flew out of the Lore City airport just before he moved to the islands. Now she had been completely refurbished with the latest avionics and looked as good as new.

Approaching the airport, he saw her sitting on the tarmac, shinning in the midday sun. As he did a quick check of the plane, he was joined by flight instructor Carrie Moore.

"She is ready to go, Riley. I took her up for a quick trip around the circuit and she is a joy to fly. I programmed the GPS for Cambridge and the airport phone number into the link sync for you. Don't forget to file a flight plan. And have a safe trip."

Taxiing to the end of the runway, Riley checked for incoming traffic. Seeing it was all clear, he gunned the engine. Lifting off the grass strip, he took one last look at the island before banking towards the northwest.

Putting on his headset, Riley filed his flight plan and asked for the latest weather update. A sharp, clear voice told him there were clouds over the mountains of North Carolina and light rain over Charleston. There was also an alert for a nor'easter blowing in from New England later. *I'll be in Cambridge before then*, he thought as he tuned in a Sirius radio station, flipped on the GPS, and engaged the autopilot.

Pouring himself a cup of coffee, Riley's mind drifted back to the time he was a kid in Cambridge at Christmas time. *Those were happy days,* he thought. *There were movies at the Strand Theater, Christmas shopping at J.J. Newbury's or Kresge's, followed by hot dogs at the Coney Island. No deadlines, stock options, or health insurance to worry about back then.*

Riley's daydreaming was interrupted by the squawk of the weather radio. Switching frequencies, he heard the broadcaster warn of the increasing speed of the nor'easter, fast blanketing Ohio with ice and snow. Gently easing the throttle forward as he crossed the Ohio River, Riley knew he was in for a rough ride home.

As he tried to find the Cambridge airport, the only thing visible was the Christmas lights on top of the courthouse. Just when he was ready to abort and land in Zanesville, Riley spotted the flashing lights on a small Piper Pacer circling low below him. Slowly descending behind him, the piper suddenly banked to the right. Following the piper as it descended into the blinding snow, the runway lights suddenly appeared out of the gloom. Throttling back, the Cessna gradually settled down on the snow-covered runway. Glancing around, Riley saw no sign of the Piper. Taxiing to a tie down area, Riley saw a man approaching to help secure the plane. That done, Riley asked, "Where is the Piper?"

"What Piper?"

"The white one ahead of me in the pattern."

"I didn't see anyone land ahead of you, sir. The airport is closed. I'm just the security man. I heard your engine and came out to see what fool was flying in this weather."

"But I saw a Piper in the pattern and followed him in," Riley replied.

Shaking his head, the man walked away, disappearing in the swirling snow.

Riley pulled his cell phone from his pocket and called his sister, Shelby.

"Where have you been, Riley? I've been worried sick about you, with the storm and all. Why didn't you call?"

"It's been a long day, Sis. Just come and pick me up; I'll explain later."

The headlights of a Jeep Cherokee appeared shortly out of the snowy night. Throwing his bag in the back seat, Riley hugged his sister as he slid into the front.

"Welcome to Ohio, Brother."

"Now I know why I live in the south, Sis."

As she drove north on Southgate Parkway, Shelby suddenly turned west on Wheeling Avenue.

"Where are we going? I thought you lived out by the hospital?"

"I want to show you our downtown area. It's been completely renovated and all decked out for Christmas with a wonderful Dickens backdrop on every corner, and a fantastic courthouse light show."

Squinting through the frosty window, Riley was amazed to see how many people were making their way through the snow-covered streets, stopping briefly at the lifelike Dickens scenes, and gazing into the store windows.

He smiled. "This is pretty much the way I remember Cambridge as a kid. Lots of people downtown. Are all these people from Cambridge?"

"Most are from bus tours," Shelby replied. "We've had over a hundred so far this year. The locals will be out for the candlelight service Christmas Eve."

Turning north on Clark Street, Shelby paused, then spoke in a low voice.

"Annie is back!"

"What did you say?"

"Annie. You know, Annie Mallet. It's Annie Janelle now. You two were thick as thieves in high school. Everyone thought you would get married."

"Annie Mallet is back in town? What's she doing here?"

"Well, her mother died last year. She came back to settle the estate and she just stayed. She fixed up the old house on North Tenth. Uh…you know she's single, don't you?"

"Annie Mallett," Riley muttered to himself. "The last time I saw her was when I left for the Air Force. We kissed goodbye in front of the courthouse just before I got on the bus. Matter of fact, it was the day after Christmas."

"What happened Riley? Didn't you two write?"

"We did for a little while, but flight school was demanding and she was in college. I don't know; we just lost contact. Then Vietnam came along. I got shot down…well, you know the rest. I wrote to her, but she never responded. I had a Christmas card from her mom saying she married a doctor."

"Well, her doctor husband decided he needed a younger wife, but she survived the divorce. And got a good settlement, I heard." Shelby paused, continuing cautiously. "I told her you were coming home for Christmas. Why don't you give her a call?"

"Is that what all this Christmas thing is about; you playing the matchmaker?" Riley smiled to himself.

"No! I just thought you might want to have a cup of coffee with her. She looks great. Go to the candlelight service with us tomorrow night, Riley; it only lasts an hour. They're having it on the courthouse square this year...please?"

"Well, alright."

As he walked down Wheeling Avenue on Christmas Eve, Riley was astonished at the large crowd. It was a happy throng of excited people.

"Half of the county must be here," he remarked to no one in particular.

Toward the end of the service, a minister spoke on the miracle of Christmas, and how everyone experiences little miracles daily. *I had mine yesterday*, Riley thought. *That fellow in the Piper was my miracle. Maybe my guardian angel.* At the conclusion of the service, Riley thought he heard a familiar voice in the background.

"Hello Riley."

Turning, Riley didn't recognize the lady in the black leather coat with the red and green scarf wrapped around her neck.

"Hello yourself. Do I…Annie? Is that you?"

"Sure is, Cowboy. Long time, no see!"

"Well, I'll be. How long has it been, uh…thirty years?"

"Well, to tell the truth, it will be thirty years tomorrow," Annie smiled.

Not knowing what to say, Riley stammered around a bit before attempting to saying goodbye.

"It's important I talk to you," Annie said as she touched his shoulder. "Can you come over for coffee later tonight, just one cup? I promise not to kidnap you."

"Sure Annie, how about nine o'clock?"

"That would be fine. I'll leave the porch light on for you."

Arriving a few minutes before nine, Riley paused on the front porch to look at the old swing they used to sit on. It was weather worn. He wondered why she kept it so long.

"I thought I saw a shadow go by the window," Annie said, opening the door. "Come in before you catch your death." The old house had been tastefully remodeled. She had saved enough of the old décor to remind her of her childhood.

"Let's sit by the tree," Annie said warmly, "we can talk about old times."

Several hours later, Riley stood up. "Wow, look at the time. Shelby will be sending the police out to look for me."

Annie touched his arm. "Before you leave, there is something I want to show you."

Reaching into a drawer of an antique desk, Shelby produced a bundle of yellowed envelopes. Turning toward Riley, she said, "I don't know why my mother never liked you. I suppose it was that old "I was Methodist and you were Catholic" thing. She never forwarded your letters to me. I found them in this drawer after she died."

Pausing to regain her composure, Annie handed him the letters and turned to look out the window. "I thought you found someone else. I don't know what to say. I'm so sorry."

Shaking his head as he read through the old letters, Riley spoke softly. "I thought you moved on. I'm sorry too, Annie," After an awkward silence, he muttered, "I better go."

As he walked toward the door, Annie gave him a quick kiss. Surprised, Riley's shaky hands fumbled for the door handle. "It's getting late. I'd better leave," he said softly, stepping out the door.

After a quick shower, Annie went to bed, finally falling asleep after tossing and turning for an hour. Startled by the phone ringing, she sat up and turned on the light.

"Hello, Annie, this is Shelby. Is Riley still there?"

"No, he left hours ago, but…where would he be? Should we call the police?"

Sharp raps on the door interrupted her rising panic.

"Hold on, Shelby; someone is at the door. Don't hang up; I'm on the cordless phone."

Annie opened the door to find Riley standing there, half frozen. Stepping inside, he stuttered for a moment, then haltingly whispered, "I can't get you off my mind, ever since you kissed me. It revived old feelings…I think I'm still in love with you."

"I never quit loving you," Annie replied as she slid into his arms, tears streaming down her cheeks.

Slowly hanging up the phone, Shelby walked into her kitchen and poured a hot cup of tea. *This is going to be a very Merry Christmas*, she thought, *a very Merry Christmas.*

The next morning over coffee, Annie giggled, "I feel like a teenager again. We used to drink shakes at the old Mecca Drive-In, now we're drinking coffee at Mr. Lee's." Waving her hand in front of him to get his attention, Annie laughed. "Hello Riley, you still here?"

"Oh! Sorry Annie, there's a picture of an old plane and pilot on the wall behind the cash register. I want to look at it."

Walking over to the picture, Riley turned to the diners eating breakfast, "Anyone know who this is?" He pointed to the picture.

"Oh! That's the Ghost of Cambridge airport," a rumpled old man in the next booth replied. "He disappeared one snowy night about 20 years ago. Never did find the wreckage. Rumor is he crashed in Salt Fork Lake."

"Really?" Riley was perplexed. "Why do you call him a ghost?"

"Well, people who live near the airport claim they still hear him flying around on snowy nights, trying to help lost pilots find the airport."

THE HOUSE OF GOLD

"Cinco, Dos, Adios! Seven Out!" was the favorite call of Seymour Scrooge. That usually meant the players at his craps table were losing, except for the few playing the Dark Side. Dollar signs gleamed in his eyes as he thought about making more money to add to his vault.

Seymour, grandson of Ebenezer Scrooge, owned several casinos throughout the world. Located in Las Vegas, Atlantic City, Tasmania, Paris, and Macau, these moneymakers were just what the doctor ordered to keep him happy. No one who saw him would realize this was one of the richest men in the world. He didn't believe in spending much money, just accumulating wealth. The smell of cold, hard cash gave him a real high.

Walking down the streets of Las Vegas, Seymour jingled the change in his pockets just to hear the sweet sounds. Neither wife nor children were a part of his life, as they would probably want to spend his savings, and that wasn't going to happen...not ever!

His casino empire, The House of Gold, extended around the world. Employees frequently complained about working conditions. Seymour frowned on raises or paid vacations. Frequent visits to his casinos assured him money was not being wasted. Visiting high security vaults, cash surrounding him, became one of his biggest pleasures. An expression he often used was "Lolly Wonga," slang meaning money in New Zealand. His addiction to riches was something he didn't want to overcome.

When he went to his Atlantic City office, Cynthia, his

secretary, gave him a message from the town of Cambridge, Ohio, asking him to attend a meeting of top entrepreneurs at the Southeastern Ohio Symposium for Global Travel. They were going to give guidance and encouragement to high school students getting ready to make their mark on the world.

"Now why on earth should I go to Cambridge? I haven't been there since high school when I lived with Grandpa Ebenezer," grumbled a stern-faced Scrooge. "That is a poor area of Appalachia. They're so poor, if they found a dollar they'd think they won the lottery. That's not a place a rich man would go."

"Isn't that the location of the Dickens Victorian Village, where the true Spirit of Christmas seems to last all year long?" questioned Cynthia shyly.

"Lolly Wonga! That *is* where they talk about Christmas all year long. Maybe this is my chance to finish the destruction of Christmas that my grandfather Ebenezer attempted. I definitely think I will make a trip to that symposium and see what I can do. My Aunt Fanny lives in nearby Byesville but I don't want to stay with her. She would expect me to pay her."

Cynthia called Cambridge to see if there was a bed and breakfast available. She knew that Mr. Scrooge would not want to stay at a regular hotel because someone might try to steal his money. Soon she was making arrangements with Colonel Taylor Inn Bed and Breakfast for a week's stay. The great weekly rate should please Mr. Scrooge.

As Seymour flew into the Cambridge Municipal Airport, he wondered how this small town could have such a big Christmas Spirit. His conniving mind worked on several plans to put an end to the Dickens Victorian Village and its holiday cheer. But first, he needed a rental car as he had several suitcases of money that he didn't want anyone else to handle.

Driving to Colonel Taylor Inn in an economical car from Cambridge Rent-A-Car, his mind contemplated where the Spirit of Christmas could be located in this friendly Dickens Victorian Village. On Wheeling Avenue, he noticed all those strange figures along the street and honked his horn at the horse and carriage just plodding along. Traffic moved slowly in front of the courthouse, with its blinking lights and loud Christmas music. *Could these things be why this is such a popular Christmas spot?*

Colonel Taylor Inn looked like a convenient place for him to stay. It was tucked away on a quiet street. The owner greeted him at the door with a pleasant, "Welcome to Cambridge, Mr. Scrooge. We hope you will have an enjoyable stay here. Could we help with your luggage?"

"Lolly Wonga! Don't need help and don't want anyone to touch my luggage. Stay out of my room. If I need anything, I will come get it," snarled the miserable, unhappy visitor. "Show me my room and leave me alone."

The friendly owners were not accustomed to this kind of guest, but tried their best to be pleasant. "If you need anything, please let us know," they told Mr. Scrooge.

After locking his door, Seymour decided to take a walk downtown. Being a little hungry after his long trip, he wanted to try the food at Theo's. Usually he had bologna sandwiches in his office or room, but tonight that wouldn't work. When he went inside Theo's, he was well pleased that he could eat there without spending too much money. *But they don't need to expect a tip.*

Heading back out into the cool night, he guessed those Dickens figures along the street looked like a good starting place to put a damper on Christmas Spirit. So, after dark, he returned downtown to play havoc with the figures. He stole something from each setting and hid the pieces in the trunk of his car. Next, he moved a few figures around. *Bet that will start some tongues wagging and people grumbling!*

But next day when he walked down Wheeling Avenue, he saw Martha, Kiyoe, and the rest of the restoration team making new pieces to replace the old ones. Men moved the figures back where they belonged. Everyone was laughing and having a jolly time. The extra work didn't seem to dampen the Christmas Spirit.

Back at the Colonel Taylor Inn, Seymour took a nap. Taking one of the suitcases out of the closet, he threw fifty dollar bills all over the bed. That was the best way for him to get good quality rest, plus he'd brought his money pillow filled with hundreds. Some people say the scent of lavender will give you a peaceful sleep, but for Seymour nothing equaled the smell and feel of money all around. Falling asleep, he plotted his next move.

In the middle of the night, he snuck down Turner Avenue to the place they kept the carriages. He thought he would find the horses there too, but Art, the carriage driver, evidently took them home for the night. So he removed the wheels from the carriages and hid them behind the Cambridge Glass Museum. *Let them look for them tomorrow*, he thought with a sneer.

Next afternoon, he heard a horse and carriage going down Wheeling Avenue. *Now how did that happen?* thought Seymour. *How could they have found those wheels so quickly? These people always seem to find a way to keep the Spirit of Christmas alive. Tonight I will fix all that.*

At the courthouse, he discovered the line that powered the lights for the evening show. *When I put an end to the music and lights, it will halt their Christmas Spirit.* Seymour never hired people to do these jobs, as that would cost him money. He used his ingenuity to cut the wires and place a remote control of his own design into the wiring. Then he would be able to regulate the lights tomorrow. Seymour smiled to himself just a little, even though it was a sinister smile. *That will fix them for sure!*

Next morning, he headed to Byesville to see Aunt Fanny. Passing Byesville Scenic Railway, he couldn't believe his eyes when he saw more Victorian figures at the railway station. *Is the Spirit of Christmas contagious, spreading to neighboring towns?*

Thick grey eyebrows gave his face a permanent scowl, which scared the children as he marched down the sidewalk waving his cane to move people out of his way. He was a shabby sight to see in his old, worn suit and short grey hair that he had trimmed with scissors before leaving Colonel Taylor Inn.

The only expensive item of clothing he owned was his shoes. Since he frequently walked long hours checking on his casino employees, he wanted his steps to be in comfort. He paid top dollar for his Berluti handmade shoes, which he purchased in Paris when he visited his casino, D'or Maison de Jeu. But, with the mean look on his face, people seldom noticed his feet!

A sharp pain pierced his forehead as he thought about the nonsense happening at Cambridge. Happiness was depressing! In his mind, money was happiness—there was no other possibility.

Traffic crawled as slow as a beginning roulette dealer through downtown Cambridge that evening. Five buses parked along the street for a great view of the courthouse lights. The chill temperature, with a few snowflakes falling, gave the feeling of Christmas in the air. Families hugged on the courthouse lawn, watching the light show and singing along to the music. Children especially enjoyed the whole Christmas scene.

Twirling around the courthouse lawn, a six-year-old girl named Holly spotted the grumpy old man as he stormed down the sidewalk. "Mom, why does that man look so sad and mean?"

"Holly, maybe he doesn't have anyone that cares about him. He might be lonely at Christmas," answered her kind mother.

Holly kept an eye on the frowning face, which carefully watched the courthouse lights. All of a sudden, with Seymour's hand in his pocket pressing the remote, the courthouse went completely dark. The music stopped and all was silent for a moment. Seymour wore an evil smirk on his face since his plan succeeded. *The Spirit of Christmas, stopped cold.*

Then on the darkened courthouse square, innocent little Holly reached up and grabbed Seymour's hand. "Merry Christmas, Mister."

Seymour flinched. But then something melted in his grumpy heart at the touch of that soft little hand. As he looked down at the blond curls, after a few minutes he said, still a little gruffly, "Merry Christmas."

Just then, the courthouse lights blinked and you could hear the song, "It's Beginning To Look a Lot Like Christmas." AVC Communications had the backup battery system in operation.

Still holding Seymour's hand, Holly joined in the singing of "Jingle Bells." With a bright smile lighting her face, Holly glanced up at Seymour, encouraging him to join in the singing. Soon both voices joined the crowd on the courthouse lawn in this familiar tune. Finally, Seymour understood the powerful Spirit of Christmas existed here due to the heartfelt touch of the people of Cambridge, very much the way his heart had been uplifted by the little girl's Christmas wish.

Ambling down the street to Dickens Headquarters, Seymour proudly announced he wanted to make a donation to the festivities. *Perhaps it is time for me to share some of my wealth with people who have a giving spirit all year long.*

"Last night," said a smiling Seymour, "I went to a play across the street at the Cambridge Performing Arts Centre. It's a beautiful old theater, but I'd like to make it a little more comfortable. Do you think they could use a million dollars for new seats and new heating and cooling?" he generously offered.

"Your town certainly does have a Christmas Spirit flowing through its streets. While it is nice to have money, I much prefer the peaceful feeling here that seems to create happiness."

Sometimes riches can't be measured in dollars and cents, but in feelings deep in the heart. Perhaps the Spirit of Christmas really is contagious!

THE GIFT OF FORGIVENESS

Sunny Clark took a sip of Chablis and wiggled her bare toes upon the plush carpet of the first-class section. They had just flown over historic Gettysburg, the pilot stated, and would arrive at Columbus International Airport in about seventy-five minutes.

Sunny reached into her open briefcase and retrieved her notes for a final fine-tuning. She had not visited her hometown of Cambridge, Ohio, since her departure before graduation night. She could not get out of that town fast enough, she remembered, and swore that she would never return. However, when the invitation to speak at the symposium arrived at her Paris apartment, Sunny readily accepted, although for less than noble reasons.

During her years in Cambridge, Sunny was known as Sandra Clark. She remembered very little about her father, as he left when she was six years old and never returned. He drank. She remembered that much. The mere sight of her provoked rages in which he called her a "useless accident" or something much worse. Sunny spent hours hiding under her bed crying, telling herself that she must be a bad girl to be treated that way.

She felt relieved when her father left, but not joyous, as her mother continued the abuse. At the age of ten, Sunny was forced to clean other people's houses and shovel snow. "You're too skinny and ugly to ever get a husband," her mother told her, "so you may as well get used to working."

High school was a nightmare. Sunny's mother refused to allow her to wear any makeup and her clothes came from second-hand stores. Her mother insisted that beauty salons were unnecessary and cut Sunny's hair herself, usually with disastrous results. In the fall of her senior year, Sunny asked her mother's permission to put highlights in her dark-blonde hair. The response was a hard slap across the face.

Home life was difficult enough, but school was nearly intolerable. Sunny's nemesis was Katie Shreve, a beautiful dark-haired fashion plate, whose greatest pleasure was to humiliate Sunny. "Nice blouse," she'd sneer. "Is it from that famous designer, Goodwill?" Then Katie and her entourage would giggle their way down the hall, leaving Sunny to fight back tears.

Katie's most painful inflictions did not require words. She simply would stare at Sunny in a way that made her feel lower than dirt.

Sunny began planning her escape from Cambridge when she was fifteen. She knew that her grandmother had left her a trust fund which she could access at age eighteen. She kept a hand-made calendar in her closet and marked off each day for three years. Her eighteenth birthday, May 22nd, was a few days before graduation. She spoke with the principal about mailing the diploma, inventing an excuse for missing the ceremony. By May 30th, Sunny was in her Columbus apartment, admiring her newly-lightened (in a salon!) hair and recuperating from a chin implant. By July 1st, she was modeling in high-end department stores. Within a year, Sunny was Europe's top runway model.

Her elbow-length platinum hair was her trademark and the legs her mother called "stilts of bone" were now insured by Lloyd's of London. Her mother was half-right about one prediction: Sunny did not have a husband. However, the tabloids and entertainment networks alerted the whole world to Sunny's list of past and present beaus, which included two professional athletes, an A-list movie star, an Italian diplomat, and a prominent billionaire.

Sunny's toes played with her Gucci shoes as she examined her notes. She recognized the man staring at her as the evening anchor for a major news network. She flashed him an obligatory smile, then returned to her notes.

Rule Number One for working overseas: Learn the language and the culture. Sunny could not emphasize this enough. In Paris, she often was embarrassed by other Americans (not only models) who expected everyone in Europe to converse in English. *Get over yourselves!* she would think. In the seven years since leaving Cambridge, Sunny prided herself in having learned to speak French fluently, and gaining some mastery of Italian. She grinned upon remembering the incident at a Milan bistro in which she mistakenly ordered "fish juice" instead of a latte. *Rule Number Two: Do not be afraid to admit your mistakes,* she jotted in a margin.

Sunny had been looking forward to the symposium with great anticipation. She would give an informative, polished speech, she promised herself. But she knew that her words would not be the lure to draw an audience. People would cram into the auditorium to see Sunny Clark, the world-famous model, cover girl, and celebrity. She fully expected the question-and-answer portion of the program to develop into a tabloid-like interview regarding her beauty routine and love life. And that was exactly what she wanted.

Sunny hoped that her teachers, from first grade through high school, would be there. She wanted to look into their eyes and say, "Remember me? I'm the mousy girl you ignored and thought would never amount to anything. Well, look at me now!" She wished to confront her mother about years of cruelty, but that was no longer possible. Ironically, her mother had been killed by a drunk driver two years earlier. Sunny wished to confront the neighbors whose houses she was forced to clean when she should have been playing outdoors. "You knew I was abused," she imagined saying, "but you did nothing but add to my misery. Well, now I have a life you can only dream of!"

Of course, there was the one person who dominated Sunny's thoughts since accepting the symposium invitation: Katie Shreve. Sunny had heard that Katie married immediately after high school, forgoing the college and career routes. She also had heard that Katie's husband recently lost his job and Katie was forced to wait tables in a diner.

I bet you aren't wearing Kenneth Cole aprons and Vera Wang uniforms as you refill coffee cups and wipe up other people's messes, mused Sunny. Katie probably would not have the guts to show up at the symposium, but it was of no consequence. The local newspaper and television station planned to thoroughly cover the event, so Katie could not avoid having her nose rubbed in Sunny's success. Revenge is so sweet, and all Sunny had to do was visit Cambridge for a couple days.

"Please fasten your seatbelts," the attendant advised. "We will be landing in a few minutes." *That means shoes on too*, thought Sunny, as she slipped on the latest Gucci's. An hour and a half later, she was driving a rented Mercedes up Wheeling Avenue.

Sunny had made reservations at the Ritz-Southgate but decided to explore the downtown area first. She parked near Theo's Restaurant. Upon exiting the car, she looked around in awe. Tour buses were in a line across the street. Life-sized characters in Victorian dress occupied every corner. *Am I in Cambridge or the Twilight Zone*? she wondered.

She tucked her trademark blonde hair into a wool hat and put on large-framed eyeglasses. *I must check this out.*

As she leisurely strolled up Wheeling Avenue, several people smiled and said, "Merry Christmas, ma'am!" *I can tell they have no idea who I am, so why are they so friendly?* She marveled at the Victorian displays and laughed aloud at a little boy who resembled a character from a Dickens novel. She had forgotten about the splendid architecture of the old buildings. "I hate to admit it," she muttered, "but I've missed this place."

Up ahead she heard booming Christmas music and saw brilliant flashing lights. *The courthouse! It's a gigantic musical Christmas card!* She laughed and applauded like a kid during a fireworks display. She even sang along with the crowd to some of her favorite carols.

She was singing "Up On the Housetop" when a "clip-clop-clip-clop" sound caught her attention. She looked toward West Eighth Street and was astonished to see two regal white horses attached to an intricate nineteenth-century style carriage. The seats were covered in red velvet and flashing blue lights decorated the wheel spokes. A man in a gray top hat brought the team to a stop. Sunny made her way to the carriage, as she had always loved horses. Three giggling teenage girls ran to the carriage and scampered in. One of them, a pretty brunette with a captivating smile, patted the seat next to her and addressed Sunny, "Come join us! There's room." "Yeah!" the other two agreed.

Sunny laughed as she climbed into the carriage. "I've never ridden in one of these!" she admitted.

"Oh, you'll love it," said the brunette. "My name is Jackie, and this is Chrissy, and Marla next to her."

"Hi!" said the two in unison.

"My name is Sandra," Sunny said, not wanting to blow her cover.

As the carriage began its excursion through the downtown area, Jackie asked, "Are you from Cambridge?"

"I lived here a long time ago," Sunny answered. "My, how it's changed!"

Their conversation jumped from shopping to boys and then to the upcoming symposium. “Are you girls going?” Sunny asked.

“Yes! We wouldn’t miss it,” clamored all three girls. “Sunny Clark will be there in person!” Chrissy gushed.

“She’s so beautiful,” added Marla. “I have a poster of her on my bedroom wall. I can’t believe she’s coming to Cambridge!”

Sunny laughed to herself at the girls’ excitement. However, the next comment threw her for a loop.

“My sister went to school with her,” said Jackie. Sunny felt a chill climb her spine. The beautiful dark hair; the slightly upturned nose—of course! She was sitting next to Katie Shreve’s little sister.

Jackie’s mood took a definite downswing. “My sister, Katie, was mean to Sunny in school. She told me how she and her friends would make fun of her hair and clothes. Sunny would never say anything back, so they tormented her all through high school. It wasn’t until just before graduation that she found out about Sunny.”

Sunny tried to hide her curiosity but quickly asked, “Found out what?”

“That Sunny had a sad, terrible childhood,” continued Jackie. “Her mother would say horrible things that no child should ever hear. She actually told Sunny that she was *ugly*; can you imagine?” The other two girls gasped in disbelief. “Katie said the other kids thought Sunny was a loner because she never played with anyone after school. Then they found out that her mom made her work at other people’s houses every day. The poor girl was treated like a slave.”

Sunny turned her head as if looking at the scenery. She was afraid the memories would make her cry.

“When Katie found out about Sunny, she felt terrible. I was just a little kid at the time, but I remember her lying across the bed sobbing, ‘How could I be such a monster?’ Sunny had no phone, so Katie went to her house to apologize. Mrs. Clark refused to let her talk to Sunny."

I never knew any of this, Sunny thought.

Jackie took a deep breath and continued. "Katie planned to apologize to Sunny on graduation day. She even bought her a small gift, a little cameo necklace. When she didn't see her at the ceremony, Katie asked the principal where she was. He said that Sunny had left town. Katie was heartbroken. To this day she is convinced that Sunny hates her. One good thing came out of this, though. Katie taught me to treat everyone with respect, as you cannot know what hardships he or she may have. That's the best advice I've ever been given."

Sunny noticed the somber faces on all three girls. Katie's lesson had made its mark.

"Is your sister planning to see Sunny at the symposium?" she asked Jackie.

"There is nothing she'd want more, but she's afraid Sunny would refuse to talk with her."

Sunny removed her eyeglasses and pulled off the wool hat, allowing her hair to tumble past her shoulders. With three young, astonished faces focusing on her, Sunny smiled and said, "Tell Katie that Sunny does not hate her. And I'd be happy to meet with her."

[illegible]

Guest Author

The Way Back to Christmas

Life's journey is a mystery that unravels over the course of decades of experience. There are times when life seems so simple and other times when the world is spinning out of control and we are caught in the tide of constant change. In our individual lifetimes, we learn that life is a cycle that carries us both away from home and then returns us to the beginning, where we find peace.

I remember the Christmas seasons of the early 1950's. In my hometown, the signal that Christmas was coming soon was the day that the city powered up the "Merry Christmas" banner draped across Wheeling Avenue at the intersection of North 11th Street. When those lights were on, we kids knew that in a month Santa would find his way to Cambridge, Ohio.

Downtown on Saturday night was a sight to behold! Lights, storefront displays, and so many people walking the sidewalks that we did not dare let go of our parent's hand. If that happened we would be carried away in the tide of humanity preparing for the Christmas celebration. Back then, major stores lined both sides of Wheeling Avenue. On the north side, businesses ran from Jack's Model & Hobby Shop west to the Berwick Hotel. On the south side was the Sohio Filling Station to the General Wholesale Auto Parts store.

Within those city blocks were many restaurants, drugstores, and all kinds of department stores. Montgomery Ward, Sears,

J.C. Penney, S.S. Kresge, Woolworths, Newberry's, and others. My parents would walk us in and out of the stores until our imaginations were teeming with visions of what Santa might deposit under the tree.

As the years went by, something called "progress" changed this wonderful world to rows of empty buildings. Some were occupied by small business people who still believed in the dream. Over the years, they would come and go like the ocean waves along the shore. Along with the disappearance of this wonderland of stores, I lost part of my past. Only memories remain of the joyful time shared with family on the old main street of this town.

Returning last year, I was amazed by the Christmas lights that danced to music on the old courthouse. People young and old stood spellbound watching and listening to the wonderful display. The city buses don't run anymore but out-of-town tour buses filled the area. Rebirth may be happening. Who knows, maybe someday the downtown will be filled with shoppers again. Parents and children may walk the streets amazed with anticipation that Christmas is coming.

Anyway, seeing the courthouse and reading of all the scheduled major holiday events reminded me of wonderful days of past Christmas celebrations.

**Our guest author is pastor of Christ United Methodist Church in East Cambridge.*

Meet the Writers

SAMUEL D. BESKET enjoys traveling and writing since he retired from Champion Spark Plug after 39 years. He is an avid reader and is a regular guest columnist for The Daily Jeffersonian, writing mostly from the blue-collar standpoint.

RICK BOOTH has authored and co-authored books on high-performance computing in the course of a software career that started with Sesame Street's earliest educational computer gaming efforts in the 1980s. He enjoys writing both recreational fiction and non-fiction history articles. Originally from Cambridge, Rick is glad to be back in Guernsey County raising his youngest son who, in turn, "keeps him young."

JOY L. WILBERT ERSKINE graduated from Air Force Brat Academy with a B.A. degree in life knowledge unparalleled by formal schooling. Her interests include foreign cultures, ancient history, the aged, and domestic arts. Writing is a passion she has enjoyed since childhood.

BEVERLY JUSTICE is a Kent State graduate and life-long resident of Cambridge. Her writing interests include traditional poetry, personal essays, and short stories.

BEVERLY WENCEK KERR enjoys weaving her tales around travel experiences, both local and afar. To create a more positive outlook on life, she shares wise sayings and uplifting words to friends and acquaintances through her card ministry.

DONNA J. LAKE SHAFER received considerable enjoyment out of writing her contributions to this book. The story line brought back many memories of Christmases past. She hopes others will enjoy our efforts as they remember holidays with their families and friends.

JERRY WOLFROM is the Rainy Day Writers coordinator. He wrote his first book, a four-page story about a race horse, when he was a fifth grader and has been a prolific writer for the past 60 years, specializing in humor and the outdoors.

The Rainy Day Writers Appreciate the Support and Talent of Mike Neilson.

Made in the USA
Charleston, SC
23 November 2012